If I'd Known You Were Coming

The

John

Simmons

Short

Fiction

Award

University of

Iowa Press

Iowa City

Kate Milliken

If I'd Known You Were Coming

University of Iowa Press, Iowa City 52242

www.uiowapress.org
Printed in the United States of America

The University of Iowa Press is a member of Green Press Initiative and is committed to preserving natural resources.

Printed on acid-free paper

ISBN-13: 978-1-60938-201-8
ISBN-10: 1-60938-201-3
LCCN: 2013934860

for adam

"She comes back to tell me she's gone . . ."

—PAUL SIMON, "Graceland"

Contents

First, for being people who unabashedly sing out loud, for believing stories are sustenance, and for their creativity, love, and support, thank you to Mark Milliken, John Getz, and my beautiful mom, Grace McKeaney. For teaching me how much a life can hold and change, thank you to my sisters, Hannah Getz and Clare Milliken. To my found sister, Emily Meier, for her uncanny insight and laughter. To Louise Jarvis Flynn, for always understanding and righting me. To the Bennington Writing Seminars, for these cherished friendships, for an unrivaled community, that vortex of relentless knowledge. For their writing, their wisdom, and for being such generous people, thank you to Amy Hempel, Sheila Kohler, Benjamin Percy, Pam Houston, Melissa Pritchard, Joy Williams, Shannon Cain, Martha Cooley, Elizabeth Searle, Robin Black, David Borofka, and Lisa Glatt. Thank you Peg Alford Pursell for so much, but especially for bringing me into the family that is MarinCo Writers. To Barbara Sturman, Melissa Cistaro, Deirdre Shaw, Danielle Svetcov, and Scott Doyle, for their thoughtfulness. To the luminous women of PAMFA, thank you. Michael Murphy, thank you. My immense gratitude to the editors and staff of the literary magazines where these stories first found homes, but especially to Mark Jay Mirsky, Christopher Chambers, Laura Cogan, David Daley, and Pam Uschuk. And to Gina Frangello and Stacy Berlein at *Other Voices*, thank you for your confidence from the starting gate. To Cedering Fox and *WordTheatre LA*. To Sally Shore and the *New Short Fiction Series*, for their voices. To my colleagues and students at the UCLA Extension Writers' Program—thank you for your inspiration! For their umbrella, the work made, and the comrades found there, thank you to the Vermont Studio Center and the *Tin House* Summer Writer's Workshop. To all the wonderful people at the University of Iowa Press: Jim McCoy, Charlotte M. Wright, Allison Means, and particularly Christa Fraser. To Frank Pichel, for the artistry of this book's clothing.

Thank you, Julie Orringer, thank you!

To Alida and Markus, who light up the world daily, gifting me with perspective and immeasurable joy. And finally, for making this book and everything in between possible, thank you to my best friend and partner in lawlessness, Adam Karsten.

Stories in this collection have previously appeared, in slightly different forms, in *Zyzzyva* ("A Matter of Time"), *Flyway* ("Names for a Girl"), *Other Voices* ("The Whole World"), *Folio* ("Everything Looks Beautiful" as "When Grass Grows"), *Fiction* ("Parts of a Boat"), *42Opus* ("Man Down Below"), *FiveChapters* ("Blue"), *Cream City Review* ("Bottleneck"), *Cutthroat* ("Detour"), *The Southeast Review* ("The Rental"), *Meridian* ("Sleight of Hand"), and *New Orleans Review* ("Inheritance").

If I'd Known You Were Coming

A Matter of Time

A hinge or a latch or some goddamn thing had rusted out and now the front door kept swinging open like an invitation.

This was when things were better than they had been, but still bad enough Lorrie was sure it couldn't get any worse. This was in Calabasas, in the five-room bungalow with the small square back porch that was partly detached, leaving a gap wide enough to catch a foot. The bungalow with the little kidney-shaped pool with the cracked floor, empty, leaving only a slick of green pointing toward the drain. This was on the other side of a head-high block wall, on the outside of a sprawling new *development* and just blocks from a mall—a mall, for god's sake. On the weekends a line of cars snaked past the front windows, waiting to pull into the mall parking lot. It was watching all those people, in their rip-sleeved t-shirts, trapped in their cars, looking sweaty, drumming their steering wheels, that made Lorrie all the more restless.

"It's only a matter of time," Marty would say. He wanted more, too.

Caroline, their daughter, had had to start kindergarten at the school on the other side of the mall. Lorrie was suspicious of the teacher; she never seemed wholly awake. And Lorrie was sure that it was not a matter of time at all, but rather, a matter of whom you knew.

So they were having friends over, *select* friends. Lorrie found recipes and wrote a questionable check for good liquor, plenty of it. Select friends and Nick Regan. They *knew* Nick Regan.

Lorrie had a knack for finding things that looked more expensive than they were, of assembling the appearance of luxury. She frequented yard sales and, though loath to be living near a mall, she bought the stemware and a tablecloth at Macy's. Through the Penny Saver she found thin bronze figurines of marching stickmen—à la Giacometti—and candlesticks and a crystal chandelier, polishing what needed polishing with toothpaste and a toothbrush, bringing it all to a high shine so as to distract the eye from everywhere else. Marty called her brilliant and kissed her forehead and cupped her shoulders in his hands, as if congratulating her for playing so hard at a game so clearly unwinnable.

They had gone to college with Nick Regan, near Cambridge, Massachusetts. Not at Harvard, but a college not far from there all the same and they'd enjoyed taking the liberty of saying they went to college *in* Cambridge, aspirating the *A*. Nick had always had a plan. If he hadn't spoken of it so often Lorrie might have thought more of his plan then, before it all panned out. In the nine years since graduating he'd produced as many films, each one doubling the previous one's budget. Lorrie learned this from the interviews she'd been reading. Now anyone could know Nick Regan as well as they did. Maybe better. This was their third attempt to have him over for dinner.

Lorrie was finishing the canapés, fully dressed—slipped into a Lagerfeld rip-off, her hair teased up and in a satin headband. But Marty was humming, still unshowered, moving through the house with a box of tools. She could smell him, his pleasant musk, wholly unfit for company. Caroline was sitting on her hands, sagged into the couch, in a depressing tulle poof of a dress, looking small. She wondered if the girl could possibly manage to keep the one outfit on through the evening. She'd been going through a phase—*for years*—of needing to wear each piece of clothing out of each drawer at least once a day. Marty found this funny, suggesting Caroline was practicing for wardrobe changes—another little thespian in waiting, like himself. Lorrie felt Caroline watching her. A pitcher of spiked lemonade was sweating on the table.

"Go change," Lorrie said, shooing her off with her hands.

Caroline fanned the dress over her knees. "You said look nice."

"Go on, please. Put on jeans. Help your dad."

Maybe Marty had this right, going about his day as he was—Nick could cancel again—but it irritated Lorrie to no end that Marty had still not dressed. She was reminding herself to hold her tongue, saying the phrase to herself—*hold your tongue, hold your tongue*—as a kind of meditative mantra. It was almost working. Their previous night's argument had ended on the admonition: *we just do things differently, Lorrie*. She wanted to be okay with this. She did. Marty was okay with it, after all. But the front door was still dropping open and sawing across the concrete stoop and back again. "Marty, please. Fix that door. And get dressed!" She was yelling. You could hear a sneeze in any room of this house as if it were right beside you. She need not yell. This too had been discussed the night before. Marty called it *hollering*.

"Next on the list," he said. He sounded as if he were underneath the bathroom sink. What needed fixing there, she did not know, but the fact that there was something more pressing than their front door made her skin hurt. She settled the last pastry into its line and lifted the tray with thoughtful arms, out to the drifting porch.

The idea was for everyone to sit there drinking and eating sticks of vegetables and small salty fingerfuls of canapés in the last of the sunshine, getting drunk, before she served them anything substantial. She wanted to relax Nick Regan, to let him know they were still fun, kid and all, and that Marty was still waiting for his break and weren't they just enough of a hard-knock story to warrant a bit of his time? Lorrie liked a feel-good story, for things to turn around. The movies Nick produced were this way. Lorrie wanted to believe it could be so easy.

They were expecting Nick, Beverly Colton and her new thing, Tad, or something small sounding like that, and an actress Marty had met in one of his acting classes, Roberta. Lorrie had warned Marty that competition, especially of the opposite sex, was not advisable. "She's fat," Marty said, to be reassuring. Lorrie smoothed the tablecloth, turned the white heirloom china—from an estate sale—and set the stemware out. Little tea lights lingered between each setting. It would be tight, six people sitting there, but they could wander in and out of the house, of course, and she was aiming for a certain level of intimacy. One of her fantasies for the night involved Nick Regan divulging some industry secret, or, even better, a personal one. Then they wouldn't have to ask anything of him tonight, then she could call him in a few days, a week later, and mention that she'd just been thinking of that little story he'd told and wouldn't it be nice if there was an audition or something Marty could come in on, they could visit afterward, have another laugh about it? This was her darkest fantasy. They, Marty, just needed a fair shot from an old friend.

Lorrie made it clear to Caroline that she could eat in her room and was to remain there after dark. They'd intended for Caroline to stay with a friend, but the friend's mother had phoned to say the girl had been sent home with lice the day before. Lice! Lorrie spent the thirty minutes after the call fingering her daughter's scalp, cursing that kindergarten teacher, but she saw no lice. And Caroline, aside from stripping down and changing outfits at every transition of the day, was a good girl, happy to do as she was told. She had always been comfortable playing on her own. They'd never considered having a second child as none of them, including Caroline, seemed in need of one. From the porch you could see into a corner of Caroline's room: she was there now, pulling through clothes, holding them up, looking for something in particular. Lorrie made a note to draw the curtains, but she didn't expect Caroline's being home to distract from the party in any significant way. Now, the last two times Nick canceled, he had had the decency to call hours ahead. But he might not this time. He could just not come, not call at all. This had not occurred to her before and something left Lorrie as she stepped back inside, realizing this. The anticipation, the flutter that was keeping her moving at the tips of her toes, the electricity at her core, turned then, darkening, like an amassing inner cloud.

She stood in the kitchen a moment, listening to Marty tinker around, then bang at a pipe on the other side of their thin wall and she knew that if Nick did not come that evening she wouldn't have it in her to invite him again. It was this evening or it was not at all and what would that be? This. She would be here, walking distance to a mall, married with child. And when someone asked Marty what he did, he would still answer: *freelance, student, odd jobs, this and that.* She hated most his answering *this and that.* She looked at the cordless phone. She pulled away her headband.

But then there he was. Early.

Nick Regan was early.

He was standing in their doorway, pulling off his sunglasses to ogle the broken, leaning door. She touched her cheeks. She had not yet done her make-up, as make-up should be applied last, so she need not step away to freshen up. A hostess must be available. She licked her teeth. "Nick Regan," she said, pushing her headband back into her hair, flattening her dress. She felt she might cry.

"Don't tell me I missed all the fun," he said, giving the hobbled door a playful shake. He had such a toothy grin. She had not remembered his teeth, not like that. He was wearing a baby blue polo shirt, the collar up, jeans and loafers. Positively put together.

Caroline came running into the room as if being chased, all elbows.

"Well, well. Who is this?" Nick Regan bent at the knees. Caroline stopped dead. The pants she'd chosen were too short and too small, pinching the round of her belly.

"This is Caroline. She was just getting dressed. Our daughter. Didn't I mention—"

"No, no. I don't think you did." Nick took Caroline's limp hand, as if to spin her around, though neither he nor Caroline moved. It was right then that Lorrie understood he was there just to stop by, to be polite, to satisfy the insistence of her many invitations, but he was headed elsewhere, somewhere better. That was why he was early. To bow out before anyone else arrived. "My word she looks just like you, Lorrie."

Caroline was between them. Yes, of course, she did have the same auburn hair, that much was obvious, but she also had Marty's cheeks—the cheeks that gave him a bit of Brando, but that left their daughter looking as if she were always about to blow a bubble.

Lorrie felt Caroline looking up at her before she even spoke, "Mom, can I go change?" A fish face.

Nick stood. Caroline turned and ran back behind the wall.

"Who knew?" Nick shrugged. "I'd have thought Marty's genes would have gone and fucked it up, but she's just gorgeous. Just like you, Lorrie." He leaned over and kissed her cheek.

"Let me get you a drink," Lorrie said. Her face flushed. He smelled of cologne and cigarettes. Lorrie was unsure when she had last eaten. The juices in her stomach were audible—only to herself, she hoped. "I wish you could stay longer, Nick." She said this as if they'd discussed his escaping already. Why skirt it? It was that obvious. "I've made an amazing lasagna, canapés. Can we have you for one drink? Gin and tonic, yes? Tanqueray? Stay for two, won't you?"

"Well, I don't eat cheese anymore. Bad for the skin. But yes, yes, a T and T will do. I wish I could stay—"

"But there are so many other things going on, of course," she said for him, waving at the air, excusing him from excuses and handed him his drink. They went on like this for a minute, with Lorrie nervously talking over him, until Marty walked in, showered and dressed, tucking in a t-shirt. He'd put his jeans back on. Good. Casual, relaxed. Nick and he greeted one another, as men do, in a sporty-back-clap embrace of sorts. She had forgotten how much taller Marty was than Nick. She'd read that it was good for an actor to be short, that the camera created the illusion of height or something. Marty was not short. But he was as handsome as he was aimless and this was what had attracted her to him. She was younger then, childless. Aimless was sexy. She'd been stupid. But after seven years they still made love regularly and she did love him. There was no getting around that.

Marty did not know that Nick was halfway out the door. She moved into the kitchen and pulled on an apron, as if there was more to be done, a larger party imminent.

"A nice place you've got here," Nick said.

Marty laughed—he was good at this part, moving people beyond any awkwardness. "It's transitional, of course. Come on, I'll show you around." He jokingly pointed in a circle, around himself. He really believed that this was just transitional. Lorrie's mother had been this way too, full of bubbling hope. It had gotten her nothing. "Come on," Marty said. They walked around Lorrie, to the back. "I'll show you the spread Lorrie's put out. The house isn't much, but we've got a sweet little space out here."

Nick flashed her a tight apologetic smile as he moved past. "All right then, real quick."

She was mindlessly wiping down the clean counter.

She dialed Beverly, wanting to tell her to hurry. Maybe he would stay if things escalated fast enough. But Beverly didn't answer. She was either on her way or picking up her new guy—he'd had his license taken away for speeding. Beverly had horrible taste in men. They weren't even handsome. Just reckless.

Lorrie went to close the curtains in Caroline's room. Caroline was down on the floor, dressed now in a blue jumper, blue shirt, blue tights, squinting at a puzzle. She looked up at Lorrie in the dimmed light. Lorrie turned on the overhead and went back to fix Nick another T and T. She poured herself a Chardonnay. Marty had given it all up. It was the new trend, giving things up, after decades of indulgence. This was right before everyone got bored and cocaine fixed it all.

Lorrie could see them through the kitchen window. They were facing the concrete wall, beyond the pool, away from her. The magnolia tree was not yet in bloom. Marty put his arm around Nick and bent toward him as if to share some confidence. She couldn't hear them, but she saw the lob of Nick's head, his shoulders rolling, as he gave into laughter. Then the two men broke apart smiling, in agreement over something. Maybe that was all. Maybe Marty had asked him for an audition, just like that. She need not fret. She stepped outside.

"This could be nice," Nick said. "Get that pool fixed up and you've got yourself something."

Marty winked at her. "Nick's excited for your lasagna, Lorrie."

She took a big swallow of wine, feeling a dribble escape onto the rayon of her gown. *Fuck.*

"My other thing," Nick started, but then paused, seeing the fresh gin and tonic in her hand. He took it and handed back the empty. "It's nothing that can't wait. I'd much rather visit with you guys. Given everything." *Given everything?* He lifted the new glass to this, toward Marty and Marty toasted him with an imaginary drink in hand.

Marty had used her, made her sound desperate for Nick to stay. Just another crazy woman desperate for a decent dinner party. That's how it was? But she *was* desperate, wasn't she? And shouldn't Marty be too? He had showered and shaved and tucked his shirt in and now he was reaching for her glass of wine. Yes, he was desperate too. Desperate enough to use her to make Nick stay. *Marty,* she wanted to say, *it seems we don't do things that differently after all.*

"I'm glad you'll stay, Nick. It's not a very cheesy lasagna anyway." She smiled at both of them and took her glass back from Marty before he could drink it. "I promise." She touched Nick's arm. He looked down at her hand. She felt a heat in her armpits. She pulled her hand back and sipped at her glass, looking to Marty, who was pointedly looking off, toward the wall. Nick fingered his ice. There was the scraping sound of the front door swinging open. Lorrie knocked back her wine.

Beverly's new guy was in fact named Tad and he was terribly small. Comically so. It relieved something for everyone. Except Tad, of course. Roberta came up the walk behind Beverly and Tad, as if on cue, a kind of punch line. She was quite fat, with a real waddle on her, thick-ankled, big drapey dress, and salty: "You didn't have to break the door off to fit me in. Way to flatter a girl, Marty." What a rag-tag bunch. Tad didn't talk much. He sat back in his chair like a sulking child while Beverly leaned forward, curled in interest over the table, just positively fascinated by what Nick had to tell of the films he'd worked on, the stories he had. Nick kept stroking his thin mustache, feeling quite sure of himself, aware of his stature amongst this group. Plus Beverly had a way of making you believe what you were saying was the most interesting thing in the world, nodding her head, mouth open as if mildly stunned by the magnitude of even your most trivial remarks. But then, when you'd concluded, she would, after a pregnant pause, blithely tell a story of far greater interest, all the while fiddling with her cascade of blonde hair. She was a gem. Priceless really, with her ability to cut people down without their even knowing. You could practically hear their knees go out. Lorrie had invited Beverly for just this reason, for leveling Nick Regan if necessary, just enough leveling to make him feel they were worth his time. Beverly had a Jack Nicholson story in her pocket. She'd met him as an extra on a comedy. She had run lines with him, among other things.

The concrete wall was lit up tangerine orange with the last of the day's light. It was the only decent part of being against that wall, the backdrop of shadows and the way it held onto the colors of sunset, like a late Rothko. It was almost cinematic. It was the only almost cinematic aspect of their lives and it was why she'd wanted everyone out here, for this light, for the illusion that they were in the world.

Lorrie had personally poured Nick three drinks by this time and she thought she saw him at the bar table inside at least once. Marty must have felt her thinking, calculating, as he reached under the table, pulled her gown up over her knee and rubbed the muscle there. He'd been telling her she was getting too thin. She didn't see it, but she liked how clean she felt when her stomach was empty. Clean and strangely full of energy.

"Right, right," Nick was saying. "I was on that picture with Jack. I remember you."

"You do?" Beverly asked.

"Jack and I are friends," Nick said. He winked at Beverly, a lazy wink, heavy with drink.

Beverly looked defeated.

Roberta had made a segue from Nicholson to Polanski and was going on about the scandal, as crude as could be, but Nick turned to her, raising his glass, "Hey, you're funny," he said. "I might have a thing for you. You got that fat thing going on, too."

"Great," Roberta said and snorted with a confident kind of pleasure.

Was he serious? Lorrie looked at Marty. Marty put his hand on top of hers, reading her thoughts as he sometimes could. Nick was getting up and squeezing behind Roberta. For a moment, Lorrie worried he was leaving, that he was laughing at them, unimpressed, and leaving.

"Can I get you a drink?" She almost yelled this.

"Getting it myself," he said.

"I blame the mother," Roberta was saying to Marty, having dropped back to talk of Polanski. Roberta was cheery faced as only the plump can be and Lorrie was filled with a fiery hate: Roberta had an audition and her mouth was positively offensive, vulgar. Marty probably found this doubly amusing given Lorrie's prudish bent. "Polanski can go fuck himself. It's the mother who ought to go to jail," Roberta said, then leaned her head back against the house as if to go to sleep. She had, up until right then, seemed oddly unaffected by four vodka sours.

With Nick inside, Tad had become awfully talkative, going on about his numerous traffic violations, all of them for speeding. Lorrie registered his talking as directed at her, as if she were interested, and wondered just how long he had been speaking to her. She thought herself rude, but quickly returned to an angry indifference. It was only Tad.

"Half the time I get off using the flow of traffic defense," he was saying.

"Oh, please," Beverly said. "That worked for you once. And it's bullshit."

"It's not bullshit. It's how it should be. If we all want to be going ninety, why shouldn't we all be going ninety?"

"He's a keeper," Marty said to Beverly.

"Like you guys are such good people," Tad said, under his breath.

Lorrie could smell the lasagna inside, the bubbling cheese she promised herself she would not touch— undoubtedly bad for the skin.

"We are good people," Marty said. "Don't be such a prick. You don't know us."

"Right up until you're rich and famous," Tad said. It took him a moment to arrange the word "famous" in his mouth. He'd had two gimlets and was nursing a wine.

"Shut up, Tad," Beverly said.

Lorrie had not intended to drink so much. "This isn't how I

thought this would go," she said to Beverly. She'd lost count of her own drinks, busily eyeing everyone elses'. "Where is he?" Lorrie mouthed to Marty.

"The bathroom," Marty said, at a normal volume.

"Please ask him already, would you? He's got dozens of things in the works. Obviously," she said, tossing her head in Roberta's direction. "Do it before he's too drunk to remember."

Marty rolled his eyes at her. She hated that. He'd gone ahead and had a glass of wine after all. The faint scent of mothballs moved off her dress.

"Marty, please."

"Lorrie, I will. Timing is everything, all right?"

The lasagna was burning.

Inside Lorrie started to pull the pan when she heard Caroline's voice. She'd forgotten about Caroline behind the drawn curtains. She did this sometimes, losing sight of her at a park, lost in her own daydream. Surely all mothers did this, sometimes. There was nothing to be alarmed over. Caroline was just talking to herself. Though not in the same way she did when pretending. When she played she spoke for everyone, without pauses, never stopping to listen, the whole story flowing freely. But she'd gone quiet now, as if listening.

Someone was with her.

Lorrie closed the oven door, quietly, and stepped into the small hallway that connected the front to the two square bedrooms and the bathroom. The bathroom door was open, vacant. But then there was Nick, around the corner, standing in Caroline's doorway, talking in a hushed tone. Lorrie thought she heard him say, "You like school?" or "You like clothes?" Through the crook of Nick's arm, she could see Caroline's still made bed, the comforter pulled taught, but the oversized pink clock on the wall had tilted somehow, leaving the 2 where the 12 ought to be. Sometimes Lorrie could hear its oversized ticking in the night, when the house was still, when she lay awake in the dark, hungry, wishing for things. Nick turned around, as if sensing Lorrie there behind him. Now she could see Caroline standing in the mouth of her closet, a pink dress in one hand, a red in the other, with only her underwear on.

"Oh," Lorrie said.

"Hey," Nick said. He was visibly drunk, the way he'd propped himself against the doorway.

Lorrie was quickly sober, sweeping past Nick. "Did you need help with that, Caroline, honey? Let me help you."

She pulled Caroline nearer the bed, where she held the girl between her knees, tugging the red dress down over her head, all the while Caroline's grunting in small, helpless protests, "I can do it. Mom. Stop."

Nick came over and sat down on the bed, right beside Lorrie, Caroline still wedged between her legs.

"She really is lovely, Lorrie. Look at that face."

Lorrie saw, as he slumped to sit, that the button of his jeans was fastened, but his fly was unzipped. A simple mistake, coming out of the bathroom. And then there was Caroline who happened to be changing, yet again. That was all. And now Nick just needed to sit down for a moment.

He inhaled deeply and set his drink on the wood floor between his legs. "I have a daughter, myself. Did you know that?" he asked.

"I didn't. No, I didn't. How old is she?" In all her reading, she'd seen no mention of Nick having a family.

"Let's see. I'm really not sure. Maybe three. I don't see much of her, of course. Her mom is, well, young. Estelle. Funny, right? An old name like that? Nothing old about her, though. She lives with her parents." Then he laughed. When Lorrie did not laugh with him, he stopped. Then shook his head. "They don't want much to do with me. *Just send a check.*"

"I see."

"I send plenty, believe me."

Caroline pulled away to push the hair from her eyes. Lorrie had been holding her arms, as if she were liable to float away. Nick reached over and touched Caroline's hair, tucking it behind her ear. Lorrie stood up, feeling short of breath. She wanted to throw open the window behind them. Marty was right there. Right behind that curtain.

"Just lovely," Nick said, looking at Caroline. "Those eyes."

"The lasagna is burning." Lorrie said. "We should go." She pulled Caroline back, by the shoulders. "We should go," she said again, to Nick. But he didn't move. He was looking at the drink on the floor, between his legs. Water was pooling beneath it, darkening the wood. It moved, ever so slightly, slipping on its own wetness. "Let's get back outside," Lorrie said. "Marty wants to talk to you."

"Of course he does," Nick said, not looking up. "I know that, don't I?"

Lorrie could feel her daughter's breathing, the small rise in her shoulders with each inhale. Lorrie took her hands from Caroline and backed away, toward the door, going. But Nick Regan did not move and a thought gathered then in Lorrie, dark and odious, just long enough for her never to forget it.

Names for a Girl

FEAR, YOUNG GIRL

Deirdre's mother folded the trailer doors closed, snapped the padlock shut, and told Deirdre to sit in the car's backseat, that it was safer there. Deirdre remembers the shimmering, golden fabric of the Le Car (her father always called it the *the* Car) and the straight gray line of street that stretched out before her like an arrow, out past all the matchbox houses. She could feel her mother and father talking behind the car, sensed their final embrace, the brief magnetic pull then repel of it.

Deirdre was thinking of the blonde-haired girl she rode home with on the bus. What was her name? She was older, nine or ten, bossy. They were always the last two on the bus. First Deirdre's stop, then the girl's. Last Friday—Deirdre remembers because it was the day her mother told her they were moving to California, that she wouldn't be going again to Mountain King School or riding the bus anymore—the girl, the bus emptied except for them, had challenged Deirdre.

"Go on," the girl said, "under your skirt." They wore uniforms: brown pleated skirts and button-down white blouses.

Deirdre slid closer to the edge of the seat and asked her to go first. The girl, without hesitation, lifted her skirt and moved her hand beneath her underwear. Deirdre watched the ripple of fabric.

"It feels good," the girl said, removing her hand, raising her arm to her face and wiping her nose on her sleeve. "Try it."

The girl put her feet up on the green vinyl seat in front of them and wrapped her arms around her bare knees, her eyes going to the hem of Deirdre's skirt. Deirdre looked up toward the driver, his sweat-stained hat reflected in the rearview. She opened her legs.

Waiting in the back of the *the* Car, made lethargic by the wet June heat, Deirdre idly slipped her hand under the elastic of her shorts. She slouched down and let her head rest on the seat, her hand moving as though stroking the neck of a cat and—not as she'd expected—she felt her body yawn, relaxing from the center out. But then, there, her father appeared, bent down and framed in the car's open window, telling her she was disgusting.

DEIRDRE

My mother told me I was named for an Irish warrior, a girl with golden hair who commanded an army of men. But now, my own belly rounding with the body of a baby girl, I am flipping through a book of names.

Deirdre: "The name of an Irish princess. Against the king's wishes, she eloped. Her lover subsequently murdered by the king, Deirdre died of a broken heart. Either derived from the Celtic Diedre (fear) or the Old Irish Derdriu (young girl)."

DEATH VALLEY

The drive took us six days and five nights. We slept in the car—to save money, my mother said, so we could stop longer and see all the places we should see: the Mississippi, the Grand Canyon, the caves in Arizona with the petroglyphs of men with raised weapons and howling dogs.

The first days on the road my mother sang along with songs on the radio, old songs, cherry-pie easy songs, letting her arm lift and dip on the wind. "Deirdre," she would say, "wave to the trucker." And I did, shuddering at the elephant bellow of the horn that followed, as if it had come from within me.

We slept in the back of hotel parking lots, pulling between trucks to go unnoticed, or settling under a tree in hopes of shade from the morning sun. But it was June and the heat always crept in first, a caress along the curve of the earth, making us twist awake beneath its warmth.

In Death Valley, I woke to the whirr of mosquitoes and the sound of my mother slapping at her own arms.

GRAPEFRUIT

The men I remember by the food, by what came with them into the new apartment.

There was one who ate sandwiches of only mayonnaise and lettuce. His lips looked loose, as if they'd been stretched from his face, then left to hang. When he kissed my mother, there was a wet, breathy sound. I would leave the room.

Another man bought bags of avocados and ate them like oranges, knifing away the reptilian skin before splashing hot red Tabasco onto their cool green sides. That man never let his legs show, always wearing thin billowy pants that looked like skirts.

One brought a bottle of wine over and cooked fish in a pink sauce that made me and my mother sweat right at the table. After excusing him, my mother complained she'd never be rid of the smell. I thought he'd been nice and silently thanked him for making us sick: we slept in my mother's bed, watched cartoons, and ate saltines for two days straight.

Paul was around the longest, so I remember his name. He ate grapefruit every morning. He cut it in half with a big knife, then took a small curved knife—with serrated edges on both sides and a dark wood handle—and slipped it down and under each pulpy triangle. He said the knife was made just for grapefruit. Knives made just for grapefruit.

MARGOT

"French. A variation of Marguerite (a pearl)." This, I remember now, was the name of the girl on the bus. I crease the corner of the page, thinking the girl adventurous and strong. Then, rethinking, knowing a memory to be carried in a name, I flatten the page back down with the heel of my hand.

NICKEL, DIME

Aidan, my father. He was in and out of the house for three years. He'd come over and spend afternoons, play checkers on the back porch, sometimes cook spaghetti with meatballs.

When I was seven, they explained about divorce. *People grow apart.* My mother and I drove back alleys, combing trashcans behind the Foodsmart and Dominick's, taking home all the cardboard boxes we could find.

There was talk of money when Aidan was over. My mother would tell me to go play outside or let me watch television so I wouldn't listen. But it was in the air, that vibration an argument leaves behind.

For Mother's Day, the year we would leave for California, I folded a piece of paper in half and drew a flower on the front. In the alley behind our house, sitting beside the neighbor's trash, I found a bowl made of thick blue glass. I brushed the dirt away, rinsed the bowl with the hose, and dried it on my shirt. In my room I emptied my bank—shaped like a pony, one hollow leg long broken off, I needed only to stand it upright for the coins to spill out. I glued them together—nickel, dime, nickel, dime—into a squat tower. When the glue had hardened, I placed the tower in the bowl, lay the card on top, and brought the gift to my mother, who was alone in the basement, taping boxes closed.

CICADAS

Paul says he's going to take my mother away on a vacation and I'm to stay with my father for the week.

I ride the airplane there alone.

When I arrive, my father tells me it is the summer of the cicadas. His body is hard and cool. I press my cheek to his chest, fold my arms around his waist as he touches my head and turns me around, moving me through the airport, out into the humidity.

The cicadas, he tells me, come once every seventeen years, breeding in cool piles of dirt, and then congregating in the trees. In front of his building, when I get out of his car, the bugs swarm and click around my head. I wave my hands and jump about, unable to stop myself from shrieking. He laughs.

He is living in an apartment with a woman who bends down when she talks to me. Her legs are thin and marked with veins that remind me of roadmaps. She likes clean children, children who wash up, fold their clothes, and make their bed. She tells me so, bent at the knees, one hand motioning, and the other holding her short jean skirt, keeping it from slipping further up her thighs. Over the woman's shoulder, my father nods in agreement, then goes to the kitchen and stands in the yellow light of the opened refrigerator.

My father works during the day, leaving the woman and me alone. I spend the afternoons outside, wandering down the street, through the park and back. I kick pinecones and find the crinkling shells of matured cicadas, the dead bodies of others.

There is a sunroom where my father grows tomatoes. Most nights he and the woman stay in their room alone. But then, once, he sits there with me, amongst the creeping vines. He gives me a coloring book and twists two tomatoes away from their leaves and slices them open, sprinkling and spreading salt over their liquid red centers. That tart flavor comes to me still on damp summer breezes.

Then the woman calls my father into the apartment.

I can see that she is agitated, her face pursed, finger waving at the couch where I have been sleeping at night and where I have perched the dead, glossy black-green cicadas, their placid eyes trained out. My father's face begins to lift in a smile, but then—the woman's voice stern, her arms crossed—I sense him bristle. He is coming toward me, his lips moving stiffly. I am nine that summer. I wrap my arms around myself and close my eyes, conjuring the buzzing swell of the cicada's song, making them rustle and swim out from the trees to lift me up.

GRAND CANYON

This, my mother told me, is where the earth opens, where men fall in.

She'd pulled the *the* Car over, the box trailer shadowing us, and we got out to look down. My mother lifted me onto the car's hot hood, explaining that this splitting of land was most likely the result of water. "Women," my mother liked to say, "are made of water."

I felt the car move first, then the trickle of dirt and rocks let loose by the shift of the trailer's wheels. She had the car started and back on the road before I could scream. When I cried I tried to be quiet, to upset no one else, but that day we cried, screaming, fearful, animal cries. She pulled into a gas station and we held onto one another across the seats.

That night, my head cradled by the seat belt, I dreamed of cliffs and small, shallow bodies of water. Then a calm glassy lake. I heard my father's voice call to me, Deirdre. I stepped out into the water and found a long strip of land divided it. I woke up remembering mud, up to my ankles, the sucking pull with every step.

When I wake up in the morning, go to the mirror, and see the pores of my nose, I pinch the skin to expel what I do not see, what is within the skin. When I do this I am thinking of Scott, the fidgety, long-fingered musician I dated in college. He showed me how he did this, how disgusting the inside of him was, how, he'd say, he could never get clean enough.

When I make coffee I use heaping spoonfuls. I like it dark, with sludgy remains after I'm finished. I used to drink iced coffee with billows of cream and sugar until Christopher insisted I taste Turkish coffee, smiling at my first wince, telling me to enjoy the flavor. So now I do.

Juan complained of the clutter on my sink. I bought a white porcelain bathroom set and separated the toothbrushes from the cotton swabs, the soap from its original container. Simple as that.

A man at work said, "Pink suits you." I bought more pink.

Michael said I mumble. I joined a Toastmasters group all the way over in Alta Vista so I wouldn't see anyone I know, driving an hour and forty-five minutes to stop swallowing my words.

Brian. I met Brian in Alta Vista and I thought that I could love him even though he was immodest. He said he couldn't come with a condom on and left when I was starting to show.

My mother liked to say about herself, wanting to be lighthearted, "I made bad choices, but at least they were handsome."

I lie in bed every chance I get and stroke my belly. At the clinic, the doctor is pale and unshaven, which leaves me wanting to go home, to crawl back in bed, to store up strength.

A girl, he says, with something apologetic to his posture.

I park in front of a hydrant, outside a bookstore, running in, engine on, to buy this book of names. I am still paging through it, still hoping to find the name for a girl without a story, without a history or a masculine derivation, a name of uncertain etymology. I will have to make something up.

The Whole World

They were in a grid of identical beige houses, against a sun-browned hillside, a muted blue sky, cloudless, still. They were stopped at a four-way stop, Bill sorting out the next turn, trying to go from memory. There was a kid's bike discarded on a weedy lawn. A dog sniffing at an overturned trash can. The air was hot and dry and smelled of horse manure, though there wasn't a horse in sight. Roxanne shifted in her seat then pushed a button that locked the doors, then another button that rolled up her window. Bill had put the top down despite her protests.

"This place is a firetrap," Roxanne said, more to the window than to Bill.

They'd been out the night before and Roxanne had stayed over at his condo in the marina. He wasn't sure why he invited her to this party—a kid's party—but he had, and now here she was in his car, in the same short black skirt and sleeveless purple top of the night before, her perfume turned tart.

It had been years since Bill had done this drive. Usually Marty came to him.

Bill pulled a map from the glove box, ignoring the show Roxanne made of moving her knees out of the way, spreading her legs apart. He wanted to keep Roxanne from asking after Marty's wife, Lorrie, so he went ahead and told her how Lorrie had taken off when their daughter was seven.

"I've no interest in children, either," Roxanne said, as if this were a perfectly appropriate response.

When Lorrie left, Marty—always lacking in imagination—was stunned. Bill had needed to stop himself from saying, "Good for her!" He asked, instead, if there was a note. No, no note, but she'd taken the car and had already been gone two days and three hundred dollars was withdrawn from their account at a branch in Utah. Utah! She really was gone. Gone and with no intention of coming to Bill.

The party was for their daughter, Lorrie and Marty's daughter: Caroline. It was her sixteenth birthday.

"You really don't have to come," Bill said again, though they were nearly there.

"Oh, no," Roxanne said, slipping her hand under the map, groping him. "I want to meet your friends."

The party was in the backyard and the kids, Caroline's friends, were standing around the kidney-shaped pool, wet and shiny, their parents perched on the edge of lawn chairs, a few mingling in the shade of a browning magnolia tree. It had to be 100 degrees. Except for the pool, the house looked more run-down than ever; the stucco was cracked open near the back door, the back porch leaned away from the house, and the pool was a touch more green than blue. Marty and Lorrie had lived in this house together. Marty refused to move after she left. The rent was too good, he said, and Caroline loved the pool.

Bill pulled his jacket off—linen, but he didn't want it getting musty. They stood at the edge of the driveway until Marty spotted them and came over, his hands full with two plates: one of raw burger patties and the other draped with wilted lettuce.

"Bill! Of course," Marty said. "An hour late is only fashionable."

"That's me." Bill took the plate of lettuce. "This is Roxanne." He motioned to her bare arm, realizing now, in this suburban context, just how low-cut her shirt was. Marty went to offer his empty hand, but Roxanne leaned in and kissed him on the mouth. This was Roxanne.

They followed Marty over to the grill, which was smoking heavily, the air thick with hickory. Roxanne slipped off her heels and moved barefoot over the grass. Bill had tried to fix Marty up, but he always refused. He was still the more handsome of the two of them: his features stronger, his shoulders broader, but he was graying more rapidly and his boyish shyness that women had once read as charming now suggested weakness. Bill was short and soft in the wrong places, but he'd learned to wear his money well. Bill was happy just to hang around with Marty and help, but Roxanne's nails were digging into his arm—she didn't want to be standing there. Bill turned, freeing his arm, and asked if she'd go fix some drinks.

"I don't know where anything is," she said.

Marty winced through the smoke and pointed the tongs at the kitchen door. "The good stuff's inside," he said. "These folks were happy there was beer." He waved the tongs toward the horseshoe of parents drinking and watching the pool full of kids.

Roxanne moved off, not toward the house, but toward the crowd. Bill knew she'd be flirting with mothers and fathers alike, looking back for his reaction, thinking this would get him. He hated this stage in a relationship—as much as he hated all the other stages.

"Good-looking girl," Marty said.

Bill shrugged. "She's all right."

"Guy like you," Marty went on, motioning to Bill's hands, "gets all the girls. Why bother settling down?"

Bill knew Marty would never cease to be impressed with his hands, even though there was nothing actually impressive about them. But Bill was a hand model, so people marveled at his hands. Really it was the money that impressed Marty, even if they both knew it was bullshit work. Bill had been *discovered;* Bill made tens of thousands of dollars for half a day's work. Fingering food, lifting soap, squeezing a lemon, if you called that work. It certainly wasn't acting, but Bill and Marty had met in an acting class eons ago. Marty still wanted to be an actor.

Bill swept sauce over the burgers as Marty laid them on the grill. "So where's Caroline?" he asked. It had been a few years since he'd seen Marty's daughter.

Marty wiped at his eyes with the shoulder of his shirt. "On the diving board." She saw them looking and waved. "She wants to be a model. I told her to talk to you." Marty was still waving back at her.

"I don't know about *that* kind of modeling," Bill said.

Caroline was beautiful. She'd been a fat little kid, but now: long penny-colored hair, like her mother's, and the same muscled body of a dancer. She clasped her hands in front of her chest, as if cold, pinching her small breasts together, before she trotted to the end of the board and dove in. She came up, her eyes fluttering.

"Listen—" Marty's tone changed, he was stern. "Don't say anything about the car. I know you wouldn't, but—"

"I know, Marty. It's a surprise."

"Thanks."

"I'm going to go fix us those drinks."

Marty was pulling the burgers off and piling them on a plate. As the kitchen door closed behind Bill, he heard Marty yell out, "Feedin' time!"

The car, Bill thought. He and Marty had been on his boat when he'd offered to pay for the car. He grew tired of Marty complaining about money sometimes and he'd been feeling good that day, his first day off after two weeks of solid work: a Pizza Hut commercial, a new Burger King sandwich, two different soda pours—one an international campaign for Coca-Cola. It was a beautiful day to be out on the boat. It had rained the week before, washing out the smog, the horizon freshly blue, two clean lines of ocean and sky forever spread out before them and here was Marty going on about what to do for Caroline's sixteenth, what a tough thing for a girl to become a woman and have no mother around—on and on. "So we'll buy her a car," Bill said, pulling in the jib, feeling like anything was possible, that she—his boat—could take him anywhere, the wind a solid gust. Marty refused, of course. He was never quick to accept. Bill had given Marty some money when Lorrie left and around a few holidays when he sensed things were tight. "But when something can be done, when there's a solution," Bill argued, "why not use it?"

"A car won't change anything," Marty said. Then, a few weeks later, he called. "Care's a real good girl, Bill. She's been through a lot, ya know? And I just—well, I *would* like to do something special for her."

They met at a car lot where Marty had picked out a used '92 Honda with a patched rip in one of the leather seats and a dent over a front headlight. "If we're gonna do this," Bill insisted, "let's do it right." They test drove a few new models, all the while Marty thanking Bill from the backseat and the chubby little salesman with his scraggly hair sitting in the passenger seat, biting at his lip, made curious by Bill and Marty's relationship. Marty wouldn't take the red one with the full package—another five thousand more than the teal green Civic with the tape deck, beige fabric seats, and manual windows. Bill understood: Marty worried Caroline would be suspicious if it were any nicer than that.

The kitchen smelled of mildew. The linoleum bubbled at the base of the sink, the faucet dripped. The cupboards flaked paint, like dead skin, and one of the doors had been removed from its hinges, exposing the drinking glasses and a bag of sugar. The liquor was still in the same place, in an upper cabinet next to the refrigerator. There was an old Polaroid, yellowed and crisp, of Lorrie and Caroline held to the freezer door by a fish-shaped magnet. Caroline looked about five or so, her face pudgy, her head leaned against her mother's stomach. Lorrie had her arms wrapped around the girl, but her face was in profile—the tip of her nose catching and splintering the sun, her eyes closed.

Lorrie had sent a letter from Texas a few weeks after she'd gone; Marty showed it to Bill. It was an oddly chatty letter. Spirited, Bill thought. She talked about the food in Santa Fe and a female gas station attendant she met in a small town north of Austin—the woman had no teeth, but smiled all the same. She mentioned news from an old friend on the east coast, a poet, but she made no attempt to explain why she had gone. It seemed clear she was glad she had and made no suggestion she was coming back, though she'd signed it, *Love Always*. Bill thought, reading it, that he understood, that he *got* Lorrie, that she'd done the only thing she could do, but he couldn't explain it to Marty. He couldn't really help him. Marty was sure she'd lost her mind and muttered that it was good that she was gone, though they both knew he didn't mean it.

Before Bill had made it, the three of them used to dress up as if they were off to some Hollywood affair, then stay in, cooking dinner together, drinking cheap liquor. Lorrie loved those first five minutes of pageantry, but over time she grew more and more distracted, busying herself with papers or looking after Caroline. Marty and Bill would sit long after the food was gone and tell stories or talk about the girls Bill was dating or if there were any auditions coming up. Sometimes Lorrie came over and sat next to Marty and ran her fingers through his hair. "I love you, famous or not," she'd whisper, but mostly she floated around them as if they were the daydream with which she could connect and then snap back from with a shake of her head.

Bill poured a shot of whiskey and drank it, looking out at the party. Roxanne was talking with two women who Bill thought looked an awful lot alike, but then realized they were both wearing the same cropped beige pants and patterned shirts. Roxanne nodded, tossing her long ponytail back and forth, as if in deep communion with them. She touched the shorter woman on the arm in some consolation. Bill figured he ought to not call Roxanne for a while after this party—let things cool off, maybe altogether.

He poured another and went to fix Marty his vodka cranberry.

There was a clamor outside the door, a rush of laughter, and three girls slid through the kitchen, slipping on wet feet, arms flailing and grabbing onto one another. One of them was Caroline.

"I have to pee way worse!"

"It's my birthday!" Caroline pushed past the other two. The black-haired one tottered, her thick arm grazing Bill as he turned around and the cranberry cocktail sloshed out onto the floor. The bathroom door slammed, Caroline inside, the other two in the hallway, dancing back and forth on their toes, dripping water all around them.

"Let us in, Caroline!"

"Like you didn't already piss in the pool!"

Bill looked for a towel. The door opened and the other girls slipped inside, Caroline striding out, more composed. Bill bent down and began wiping at the floor.

"Hey, Mr. Morse," she said. She remembered him.

"Happy Birthday, Caroline," he said to her bare legs, as she stepped through the backdoor and out onto the lawn.

Bill saw Lorrie naked once. Marty had gotten a bit part as a teacher on *Diff'rent Strokes*. They had people over that night to celebrate, sending Caroline to sleep at a friend's. The party was a small group that got drunk too fast and bored easily. They started playing cards, which unavoidably turned to strip poker. Marty passed out barechested, still wearing his pants, on the living room rug. Intoxicated, Bill had to stop himself from staring at Lorrie. She sat as straight and proper as an Englishwoman, her breasts snug in the crook of her arms, her cards fanned out in front of her.

Bill was winning. He still had his shorts and socks. Lorrie's underwear were the last to go, and everyone scurried out back to go swimming, to feel the slip of each other's skin in the dark water of the pool. Lorrie pushed back from the table and started to gather empty bottles from around the room. "What do I win?" Bill asked.

"Oh, Bill," Lorrie said, "don't be common." She was comfortable in her skin. "At least ask me to dance," she said, not turning to him, but spinning around from one end of the counter to the next, her hair twisting like red ribbons.

Bill couldn't move. He was too drunk, his erection too obvious. He stayed behind the table, pathetically concealing himself. She stopped at the sink, setting a glass down, and stared out at the yard, at the bobbing heads in the pool, her back to him, her body suddenly melancholy. There was a small diamond of down at the base of her back, a shimmer of fine blonde hair. Bill watched her foot arch up and down, the indent of her ankle flex thin. Then she turned back and came toward him. She started to gather up the cards that lay scattered across the table. He wanted to touch her breast. He began to lift his hand, just as one would unconsciously reach to touch something made of silk, but was then jerked awake and laid his hand on hers instead. "I love you," he said, his words more steady and sure than he had anticipated.

"And I you," she said back, friendly, an awkward half smile.

This was the same summer she left.

"No," Bill said, letting his eyes meet hers. "I love you," he said again, wanting to reassure her.

But she was angered. "Let me go, Bill." She turned, the screen door smacking shut.

A haphazard line snaked from the barbeque, mostly parents with a few of the heavier kids tucked into towels and snorting amongst themselves. Marty was forking burgers and shaking them onto people's plates. Roxanne stood talking to him with one long-nailed hand on his shoulder, the other at her hip as if she were a model at a trade show trying to sell him the grill. She was actually an aid to an entertainment lawyer who, Bill suspected, she slept with occasionally. Bill and she were not exclusive and it had been plainly stated that she had started seeing Bill to spite a former girlfriend of his who had once spited her. Bill appreciated the honesty. He handed Marty his drink and Roxanne gave him a pouty look, as if to say, Where's mine? He pulled a beer from the cooler under the table and handed it to her.

"Hey, why don't you show them how the pros do it, Bill?" She was motioning to the condiments, the burgers.

"Yeah," Marty chimed in, "show us how it's done."

They couldn't be serious. Bill swirled his whiskey and drank.

"That's who you are," a short wiry-haired woman, two-parents deep into the line, said. "The hand model." She'd been fanning her empty plate at her face, warding off the flies that had begun to gather. She handed her plate to Bill. Marty loved to tell people what Bill did for a living.

He offered his hand to introduce himself. "Bill Morse," he said. But the woman shook her head and made a shooing motion. Once people knew what he did, they got strange about his hands, as if they were on fire or broken.

"Lemme get a look at those," the balding father at the front of the line said. Bill spread his fingers, hovering over the pile of buns. "Nothing special, are they?"

"Insured for a million dollars," Roxanne offered.

A mother gasped.

"A half-million," Bill clarified, and then felt stupid, as if that made it any less ridiculous. His agent had talked him into it when he'd gotten overbooked last year—having to reschedule a noodle job in Japan. "That," his agent said, "means you've really made it."

One of the father's peered over the table. "They're feminine, aren't they?"

"He did a Palmolive ad once, didn't you?" Roxanne said, smirking. This wasn't true.

"I don't do full hand. Mostly you see the tips of my fingers. Never the palm of my hand or my wrist." People bunched around closer, like a science fair. Bill set a bun onto the plate, open-faced, and added the crispest piece of lettuce he could find, setting two tomato slices onto that.

"Shall I burger you?" Marty asked, forking a graying slab.

Bill waved him off, and took up a spatula and slid the burger patty down, without moving the tomato, saying, "It's really all about manual dexterity." A few hums of understanding came from the women. "It's being able to pull the piece of pizza from the pie at the same speed and with the same tension of cheese for every take."

"Or pouring soda without that foam," the wiry-haired woman said, nodding.

"That's right." Bill placed the cheese squarely before picking open the caked hole in the top of the squeezable ketchup bottle.

"No onion?" Roxanne asked, in mock alarm.

"Onion can be polarizing. You won't see much onion in sandwich advertising—puts some people off." He set the plate down and swirled a curve of ketchup and mustard—both at once—and capped the bun.

"Masterful," Roxanne said. "Artwork."

"I don't know," the wiry-haired woman said. "It doesn't look good."

Bill shrugged and pawed chips from the bowl. "The food stylist makes it look good. I'm just the timing."

"I knew a food stylist once," the bald guy said. "They spray shit on the food."

"Something like that," Marty said, smiling at Bill as if in cahoots.

Bill had tried to teach Marty about lighting, bringing him to his jobs, introducing him to the grip and gaffer, hoping to get him work as a best boy or operating the dimmer board, at least. But he didn't seem to appreciate the technicalities, never remembering what kind of light they'd used or how one differed from the other. But demand for Bill's hands was high enough that he could guarantee Marty a few days of work as a PA on most of his jobs. Driving a truck around, picking up equipment and dropping it off when they were done—it was the low rung, a college kid's gig, but Marty didn't seem to mind, always excited about the craft service spread of free food. He'd been the finest actor in their acting class. Charming, handsome, abandoned Marty. Marty was owed what Bill got him and then some.

They gathered to eat on the leaning-back porch, a small group breaking off to balance on the raised roots of a magnolia tree. Bill sat on the low railing and Roxanne folded her legs beneath her and leaned against him, picking at a pile of pickle slices. Well, aren't we cozy, Bill thought.

"Do they use real cheese on the pizzas?" A father asked, mouth full.

"It's the law," Roxanne said. "They have to use the same ingredients they use in the restaurant."

People nodded and chewed.

"Go eat!" the same father yelled over to the pool, where a few kids were still splashing.

Bill turned around to see Caroline, still in her bikini, sitting at the end of a lawn chair, a group of boys and girls at her feet. A tall blond-haired boy with the beginnings of a mustache sat down behind her. He began kneading her shoulders.

"That's Raymond," Marty said, answering to the raised eyebrows. "I don't know if he's trouble or not."

"He's cute," Roxanne said.

"His parents here?" Bill asked.

The woman who'd pulled her glasses from her purse to inspect Bill's hands said, "Nope. Lives with his dad. He's a drunk."

"Caroline doesn't seem too interested," someone attested.

"She's a good kid," Marty said. Everyone mumbled agreement.

The bald dad raised his empty beer bottle. Marty asked Bill if he'd help carry the cooler to the porch.

"How do you think it's going?" Marty asked, as they passed the pool.

"Plenty of food, the kids are having fun, and the parents seem comfortably drunk."

Marty pulled on the cooler, getting a grip. "They've all helped me out in some way over the years."

They bent and lifted.

"Sure," Bill said. He caught Caroline out of the corner of his eye: a backlit silhouette, her arms were raised above her head in a playful pose, one leg bent, like a ballerina. Raymond jogged up and pushed her in. She screamed, a high, excited scream, and her hair whipped up behind her before she broke through the surface of the water. Bill saw Marty smile, watching too, and then his eyes shifted.

"But not like you," Marty said. "Nobody has helped like you have, Bill."

"Stop." Bill shook his head and adjusted his grip on the cooler. "It's not necessary."

They set the cooler down on the porch step. Marty swung the lid open and Bill tossed the bald dad a beer. "Heads up."

Marty passed the rest of the beers around, handing off the bottle opener. "We'll do cake soon. Then the car," Marty said, motioning toward the garage. "I'm excited about the car. Are you excited about the car?" Marty was talking out of the side of his mouth, a half-whisper directed at Bill.

The car? Was he excited about it? No, Bill realized, he was not. He pictured Caroline wrapping her arms around Marty. "It'll be great," Bill said. "She'll love it."

Marty handed him a beer and Bill forced it into his back pocket, the moisture seeping through his jeans. Roxanne was flirting with the bald dad, her legs crossed, her ankle grazing his.

Marty looked at Bill. "Guy's going through a divorce. His wife was here earlier. That didn't work. I can tell him to cool it," Marty said.

"It's amusing," Bill said.

"You're a stronger man than I."

"Something like that." Bill started to gather people's empty plates, but a few resisted, still eyeing his hands. Roxanne noticed and consoled them, telling them about his manicurist, the bottles of lotion he kept in the car, even the fucking knuckle waxer that Bill could and should pitch in because his job was for assholes. "Thank you, Roxanne. Thanks for explaining that," Bill said.

He balanced the plates he had over to the garbage. The sky was washed pink and orange and the temperature had dropped to a tolerable level. Bill dumped the armful into the lidless utility can, thinking it looked like something Marty might have fingered from a production set. The folding table, with the food on it, looked familiar too. Marty had the opportunity, being the one to close up the sets and drive things back to the rental and production houses. Not a big deal, Bill thought. We all take something here and there.

He pulled the beer from his pocket and leaned against the wall of the garage, thinking he'd take a minute and drink by himself.

"Can I get a sip of that?" It was Caroline. She'd put a t-shirt—several sizes too big—over her bikini, leaving a wet imprint in the fabric.

Bill looked at the bottle, then past her: the parents, Marty, and Roxanne were still on the porch, blocked from view by the magnolia tree.

"Sure," he said, shrugging. "One sip. Consider it my birthday present." He handed her the beer and she opened it, sideways, against the doorframe of the garage's side door. "Nice trick," Bill said.

"Betsy taught it to me. She's the big one." She pointed toward the house, suggesting their meeting in the kitchen. She gulped at the beer and it fizzed and popped.

Bill leaned back and crossed his arms. She had more freckles than Lorrie, her hair was darker, almost brown.

"Do you remember what you told me at Christmas?" she asked. Bill hadn't been to their house for Christmas since she was eleven or twelve—the last time he was probably at the house at all, the last time he'd seen her, he figured. "You told me," she said, "I would be more beautiful than my mother someday."

"I did?" Bill remembered now. He had said that. He'd been drunk. He looked at the ground, at Caroline's feet, at her toes kneading back and forth at the dirt at the edge of the lawn. He always got drunk in Calabasas.

She fingered the lip of the bottle. "And now I am," she said. She smiled a thin, devious smile. Her eyes narrowed at him. "You wanna see my new car?"

Bill startled, his hands went out. She grabbed him by the arm and opened the side door. *What an idiot,* Bill thought about Marty. She'd already found the damn car.

"Voila!" she sung, with a sweep of her arm.

One Honda Civic. Paid in full. She opened the driver-side door and motioned for Bill to sit down, bending in a curtsy.

"This was supposed to be a surprise," Bill said.

"My dad's horrible with surprises. He showed me days ago. He told me to act surprised. Like it's a big deal."

"It *is* a big deal." Bill said, lamenting his own fatherly tone. She slid into the passenger seat. He pulled the beer from her hand and took a swig. She'd nearly finished it.

"Hey," she said, grabbing it back, "that's my birthday present."

He let her take it. He should have brought her something, something wrapped. She was pretty, but more awkward than Lorrie, with Marty's chin. He wished he had another beer, for himself—a prop to hold.

"How about a drive," she said. "Just the two of us."

"Right," Bill said, gripping the bottom of the wheel.

"How about right now?" She opened the glove box and pulled out the keys.

"Cut it out," Bill said, his voice breathy, a near-shout. She was making him nervous. "Christ."

She tugged at her t-shirt, pulling it lower on her thighs.

"My mom took the car when she left. Did you know that?"

This was true, they had only the one car then and Lorrie had taken off in it, leaving them stranded, Marty having to ask people to pick Caroline up for school. At first, Bill had given Marty the money for a rental, then a replacement. "A loan," Marty had said. That's two cars, Bill thought. Two cars, he'd bought. Both cars.

"What if I told you I paid for this car?"

She was finishing off the beer. She covered her mouth, concealing a burp. "I'd say you were a liar." She turned toward him, meeting his eyes. "I'd say you were trying to get in my pants."

"I am not!" he said, his voice spiking like some pubescent boy. What a brat, Bill thought, what a little brat. Lorrie would never be so abrasive. She did make him think of Lorrie.

"Let me see your hands," Caroline said. She pulled his right hand from the wheel, fanning and studying the fingers against her thigh.

Bill flashed on what she looked like years ago, that kid in overalls. "You really remember me?" he asked her.

"My dad talks about you all the time. You're his big movie star friend. He's always pointing out your hands on TV."

He felt the tips of her nails running along the lines of his palm. "I'm not a movie star. I mean, I don't know. Does your dad talk about your mom?"

"Sometimes." She folded his fingers inward and stroked his knuckles. "Why?"

"Just curious," Bill said. There was a rack of wrenches on the garage wall, a loop of rope, the lawn mower hung awkwardly up on one rusted hook.

"You want to kiss me," she whispered.

"Does Raymond kiss you?" The skin of his arms went prickly, alive.

"He's just a boy," she said. Then she leaned over and brushed her mouth against his neck. "You like that," she said, her words made little puffs of air in his ear.

"I *did* pay for this car."

She sat back and let go of his hand, her body suddenly rigid, "You mean because you get my dad work? Is that what you mean? I know that. I know that you do that. You paid like that?"

"No," Bill said, "I paid for it."

She was quiet, thinking. "I guess that makes sense," she said then. "My dad's pretty much useless."

"Hey. Your dad makes good money." Bill pulled the empty bottle from between her legs and let the last slide of fuzzy beer drop into his mouth. "He does fine."

"Please. He talks like he does." She reached out and turned the dial on the radio, clicking it back and forth, absentmindedly, no power, the car off. "He cuts coupons, you know. It's like he doesn't care. Like this is good enough. All of his clothes are used." She put her feet up on the dash—small, thin, lovely feet, the toes edged with dirt. "My mother's clothes, too. I remember that. That odor. She told me she hated it. Walking around in someone else's smell."

"Your mother was a beautiful woman." He would have taken great care of her.

Caroline shifted toward him, her whole body, her knee on his thigh, her ankle curved against the parking brake. He thought she was going to crawl into his lap. He looked at her. Her eyes were filling with tears, her lashes damp and gathering together.

"You're beautiful, too," he told her, his voice once again unsteady.

"Why'd you tell me that?" She wiped at her cheeks and swallowed.

"I don't know," he said. "I wanted you to know I'd gotten you something."

She shook her head, "I know I'm not beautiful. Not like her."

Bill touched her arm. "You are," he said.

Outside there was laughter. A boy's voice called out "Marco," followed by a girl, "Polo." He kissed her forehead, her skin smelled of chlorine and sunscreen.

The first job Bill had gotten Marty was a Pop-Tarts commercial. After they'd wrapped, Marty got the entire crew to sing to him, "He's got the whole world in his hands, he's got the whole wide world." Every single one of them—from the AD to the pimple-faced PA—going along with it, but at the same time they were all snickering at the lunacy of this, at Marty's display of gratitude. Bill took him out for a drink afterward, waving everyone else off. "I know you loved her, too," Marty said then. "Of course I did," Bill said back. They'd let it go at that.

Bill looked at Caroline's thighs, the strong tan curve of her muscle against the fabric seats. He put his hand back on her leg and squeezed gently. She was quietly crying, her face splotched with red when she looked up.

"You're *more* beautiful," Bill whispered.

She wiped her eyes with the hem of her shirt, then put her hand on top of his, holding him there, against her thigh.

"I was looking at one of those magazines yesterday, with the really outrageous stories—"

"A tabloid?" He adjusted himself in the seat, awake to the shift in her tone. She was still holding his hand against her thigh, against the fine hairs there.

"Yes, a tabloid," she said, looking at him crossly: don't interrupt. "The front cover had this enormous woman. Big and fat. Rolls and rolls of flesh," she said. She let go of his hand and began braiding the wet strands of her hair.

"Uh-huh," Bill hiccupped. He did not move his hand away, but kept his palm still and solid.

"The headline said, 'Woman Eats Entire Home.'"

"Wow," Bill mumbled, watching her mouth, the lower lip more prominent. He was allowing his fingers now to sweep back and forth over her skin.

"The article said she ate her husband first, then the kids, then the furniture and the house. From the inside out."

"Hungry lady," Bill said, his mind fixed on the freckles that dotted the arch of her cheeks, her hair now slicked away from her face, and her legs—the feel of the skin as soft and warm as bread.

"It made me think of your commercials," she said, and touched his knee. "How the food looks all big and perfect. How it's larger than life and it makes people really want it. They're really, *really* hungry, watching. Wanting everything. Craving it, you know?" she was talking eagerly, her eyes wider, animated.

"That's the idea," Bill nodded.

"And then your hand comes in," she lifted Bill's hand up off her leg and looked at it. She began moving it up and down through the air, "and you're dipping the sandwich or pulling at a fry and all of a sudden the food isn't larger than life. It's just a regular old burger in this regular old hand. Just Bill's hand."

He pulled away and shifted the bottle he'd wedged between his thighs. He was aroused. He could feel her staring at the side of his face, her hands twisting the braid at her neck, round and round.

"It must be hell for you," she said, "disappointing people like that."

He didn't want to be aroused, but he was. He didn't want to be drunk. "It made you think all that?"

Outside someone called for Caroline. She turned toward the door, then back to Bill, her body a flux of nervous energy.

"That," she said, "and how much I hate my mother." She had her hand on the car door, but then she stopped. She leaned over and she kissed him—wet and openmouthed. "I think I feel sorry for you," she said, pulling away.

"Caroline?!" people were yelling.

When she kissed him like that, he brought his arms up around her waist. She was within his arms. He was holding her. She reached for his door handle now, half in his lap as she was. He was holding on. "Please don't go," he said. He kissed her again, her neck, her chin. Finding her mouth, he thought he felt her kiss back, but he was most focused on his hands: the necessary grip, the measure of pull in his forearms, the tension, sensing his knuckles going white against the sound of the garage door opening, the thrust and clack-clack of it, and the thin pink light of dusk falling in on them.

"Let me go," she said, her hand flying to his face, her legs kicking, the car's interior light coming on, her body slipping from him, over him and out the driver-side door.

"Bill?" Marty's voice.

Then the crash of a platter onto concrete, followed by a fidgety silence, the din of a gathered crowd before he heard Roxanne begin to laugh.

Everything Looks Beautiful

On Tuesdays the gardeners come and Lila puts on the cowhide skirt. She likes the feel of the tanned leather, the smooth slip of it across her legs as she dances. She dances to mariachi music.

There is the sound of the mower on the front lawn and Lila goes to the bedroom, dresses, opens the windows and then draws the curtains. The curtains are sheer and white and she is sure—once the gardeners come around to the backyard—that they can see the sway of her hips, the twist of her silhouette behind the fabric. She turns the stereo up loud enough for them to hear over the mower and the trimmer.

The backyard usually takes three songs and by that time Lila is damp with perspiration and short of breath.

She goes to the kitchen, fills three glasses with ice, and balances the pitcher of lemonade outside. She lets the gardeners help themselves, seeing it makes them feel more at home. Roberto is the tall one, with a mustache. And the little skinny one's name is either Santo or Sanso—she has never heard him properly. The three of them move to the end of the brick walkway and look out across the yard, watching the sprinkler wave a wide smile back and forth over the grass, drinking together, thirstily.

"It's almost time to cut back the persimmon tree," Roberto says.

"Not just yet," Lila tells him.

She likes to watch the sprinklers most on sunny days when she can catch the flash and dispersion of little rainbows beneath the water's stream. Tuesdays have become Lila's favorite days—the smell of fresh-cut grass, the stiff odor of the sweat of these men, and lemonade.

"We're due next door," Roberto says.

She writes them a check, adding, "Everything looks beautiful."

"Gracias," Santo or Sanso says, raising his empty glass.

Lila doesn't dance for Paul. It isn't the same. Paul has no legs, or hasn't for over three months now, and he doesn't seem to miss them. It is as though he has always been in a wheelchair, as though someone just came to the door one day, a messenger boy in khakis who pointed to Paul's knees, saying, "I'm here to pick those up," and Paul only shrugged and handed the limbs over. He still plays basketball with his friends on Saturdays—everyone ignoring when he rolls over their toes. He still goes to work, with a new higher desk. He even got a raise. He insists they should start a family, as planned, within the year.

Lila pictures a baby pulling itself along the floor with only the strength of its arms.

Lila asked the doctor where the legs went even before she'd thought to find out how Paul was doing, if the surgery had gone *as planned*. Some plan. Paul had offered the legs to science. "Such a good man," the doctor said, to which Lila had almost responded, *Really thinks on his feet.*

The driver who came sailing through the farmer's market, pinning Paul—knocking him down with the front of the car and holding him still with the back tires—was eighty-five years old and had driven the same maroon Buick LeSabre clear through his own garage door one week earlier. After he'd come to a stop—seemingly wedged still by Paul—Lila helped the old man out of his car. Three other shoppers pushed and rolled Paul free. The ambulance took too long, the blood clotting at the thigh, the feet and ankles dying without pain.

Lila wondered if she would feel less, less of lessness, if Paul had been a soldier at war or a racecar driver flung from the track, if he'd been an active participant in his own tragedy.

One other person had been hurt, not so badly, but an elderly woman had a heart attack after the fact and died on the spot.

"Maybe I had a stroke," the eighty-five-year-old man said to Lila.

"Or maybe not," Lila said.

Paul has started going to the market again, the city having constructed six-foot wide, three-foot deep cement barricades that are now towed in and out of place every Sunday.

Being some brand of celebrity there, Paul comes home and shows Lila what he's been given for free: two mangos, an orchid, a sack of organic potatoes, and a bag of walnuts roasted in red chili powder.

After dinner, as is the new routine, Paul wheels the dishes over to the dishwasher, sets them in the rack, and rolls toward their room. But Lila stays at the kitchen table and unwraps another baked potato from its foil, squeezing its insides out. She does not eat it, but watches the navy blue of night change it before her eyes. A wonderful, free potato.

Paul is in bed. The lights out. They have touched and kissed and curled against one another, but they have not returned to making love. Lila knows this is because of her more than him. She takes off her shirt, her pants, and slips behind him, under the sheets.

"I'm not dead," he says.

She reaches down and touches the mottled flesh, the petals of scar tissue around what was once a knee. "What does it feel like?" she asks, her hand still.

"Like my legs are gone."

"That's all?" She moves her hand away.

He rolls over to face her. This is where things have always stopped—with his deep brown eyes on her. How can nothing else be different? Why are his eyes not now blue? How can he look at her as he always has?

"I'm not dead," he says, again.

Lila rolls away, out of bed. "Music," she says, and opens the windows and turns on the stereo. "I'm going outside," she says. "You can watch me or not."

The trumpets are fainter, the guitars more distant, but as Lila moves she knows—even if he cannot see her in the darkness—that he can feel the twist of his ankles, the flex of his calves, and his feet mashing down the wet, green grass.

It is Monday. This is as high as the grass will ever get.

Parts of a Boat

The boat is quiet except for the clanking of the halyard against the mast. Catherine edges herself down from the bunk and moves to the head, to wipe the crud of sleep from her eyes. She is still resolving herself to the horror the small, round mirror has revealed—her hair smashed, her face lined with sheet marks, her mascara—when the harbor dog, Buoy, starts up barking, followed by the quick, clipped footsteps of a woman on the dock. The boat leans starboard: the woman pulling herself aboard. Roxanne.

"Have we got a good one for you," Roxanne says. She is bent down in the boat's companionway, a short blood orange dress frames her breasts—breasts as pert as if she were upside down.

Catherine eyes her wrist, her bare wrist: Bill having removed her watch while she was sleeping. His small niceties are equally considerate and inconvenient. "You're early. I think."

"No. We're late," Roxanne says, already down the steps. "We're always late," she says, as if late and fabulous are equivalent.

Behold Roxanne: hopping on the balls of her pedicured feet, red-ribboned sandals dangling from one tan, thin arm, the other weighted in a dozen golden bracelets. She is a well-heeled forty. Looking twenty. Catherine can't help but hate her.

Roxanne's husband, Sean, follows with a canvas bag chinking at his side, announcing its liquor contents. He hefts the bag to the counter and leans in to kiss Catherine. "Looking good," he says. He hasn't looked at her. He is a disconcertingly handsome man, as if he were wearing makeup. Could that be? Yes, yes it could.

Catherine has had dinner with these particular friends of Bill's only once before, a year ago, not long after moving in with him. Neither Roxanne nor Sean had paid her much mind then and Catherine hadn't held it against them. Plenty of women had passed through her chair, maybe even Roxanne. They'd been to an overcrowded Asian fusion place. Catherine needing to lean in to make out what was being said, lingo she didn't yet understand, all the talk centering on Sean and Bill, their careers, naturally. Castings. Shoots. Who was Catherine anyway? Just a single mom, fresh off a moving van from the Midwest. And already lucky enough to be eating lettuce cups with Sean Max, the actor, and his striking wife, Roxanne. Roxanne had had work done, of course, but it was good work. Then, waiting on dessert, they ran through the usual questions about Catherine's move from Illinois, the litany of expletives about the weather, how relieved she must be and all of that. It was a subject she tired of quickly. She was here now. Why speak of old lovers?

"Where's our Captain?" Roxanne says. She is flush, tan and flush. She maneuvers around Catherine, toward the unmade bunk, where she lifts herself up and settles on their strewn sheets, crossing and bouncing one bird leg against the other. "We have such a wicked little story," she says. The boat feels narrower now, crowded with Roxanne's taut good looks and gameshow energy. Bill has yet to return.

"He's gone to the store."

"We have to wait for Bill," Sean is saying. "Cath doesn't want to hear the story twice."

Cath. Good then. They're already the best of friends.

Coffee, she needs to drink a tanker of coffee.

She and Bill had spent the afternoon on the boat, leaving her son, James, at home with the woman Bill hired. The two of them needing a break from *the family life*—Bill's phrase—from time to time. And she *is* flattered, his wanting her all to himself more often. Yet away from her son, Catherine feels a low-grade sort of panic underneath everything; James needs her, or she needs him, or she needs him to need her. A hollow vibration in the bones. Yet something still quieted by a glass of Pinot in the mid-day sun. They finished that bottle over a game of backgammon. She wasn't really even trying. She'd let Bill trap her runners before she'd moved any points at all. The game was inevitably over and then Bill offered to adopt James. Just blurted it out. *A father would help* or something like that, referring to the fact that James didn't speak, that he had recently stopped speaking altogether, even to the speech therapist. Sessions Bill was paying for three days a week, sometimes more. But it was disingenuous, this offer, the effort. Bill always moved around James, her now silent son, skirting him, as if the boy wielded an invisible weapon. This talk was all bravado. Game-induced bravado, clear in the way his eyes never left the dice. They *were* drinking. She opened another bottle, considering a response. She was more aware than usual that Bill was no taller than her, shorter even. They argued, briefly. She crawled into the bunk. Thoughts of her son in this drunken afternoon and the reminder of his dead father, her dead husband—she had reached the last leg of some emotional triathlon. She was spent. And with the steady clap of water all around she drifted into a deep sleep, only to wake alone. A note on the counter: *We need more shrimp. B.*

And now here were Roxanne and Sean and this threat of a story.

On shore, Buoy starts up with his raspy warning bark again, alerting the entire channel to anyone's arrival. Roxanne exhales and quickly draws a sharper breath in, as if to calm herself. She is grand in all her expressions. A birthing kind of breath; though she is, of course, childless. Childless women. Catherine's mother had told her she would never see childless women the same after having a baby. She'd thought this meant she would think less of them, but sometimes there was also an unquenchable envy.

Bill's abrupt, hurried footsteps are on the dock. Then aboard. "There are those beautiful kids," he says, looking down into the cabin.

"Bill!" Roxanne spins and leaps toward him, even as he is still easing himself down the steps.

Bill loves company. Loves people. Maybe even Catherine. Maybe she loves him. Or wants to be more like him, to have his ease and whimsy around anyone. It is the latter, but they could get there, to that capital L kind of love. "I mean, why not?" Catherine once remarked to an old friend from Illinois who paused too long before responding.

"We've got such a good story for you! Blood and gore and everything!" Roxanne is saying. She has Bill's face in her manicured hands.

After that first dinner, Catherine asked Bill if he and Roxanne ever dated. He assured her they hadn't, but he'd been curt with Roxanne that night, sharp, as if they'd reluctantly made-up from some heated argument.

"Fabulous. Blood and gore? Let's save it for dinner then, shall we?" Bill shares a wink with Sean, "Drinks first." Sean is dropping olives over chipped ice.

And then comes that thin pane of glass between her and them—this is how she has described the feeling to Bill. It goes up and she is behind it, trapped in a familiar remove. She is handed a drink. Everyone is smiling. The cabin fills with the hard paint smell of vodka.

Catherine and Bill met at a bar. She had brought James to Los Angeles only three days before. She'd left James asleep in the motel room, alone, the door locked, a simply worded note beside him. She'd been lying awake for hours. She needed company. Adult company. Conversation. Someone who could hold *her* hand *in his*. Bill did not fault her for this.

"I'm in commercials." This was how he introduced himself. It was perfect, exactly why she'd come to Los Angeles. Fantasy as fact. "A hand model," he said, looking at his own hands. "Some bit parts, too, character acting," he said, shrugging his round frame. But he was the first man, let alone person, that she met in L.A. and she felt like she recognized him and that was comforting, the false sense of déjà vu. Like returning to a dream from which you'd been rudely awakened.

"He's only six years old, for fuck's sake. Who does that? Who leaves a boy like that?" she kept saying, needing to get back to James, sliding against Bill's parked car, after the bar had turned on all the lights and asked them to leave.

Roxanne goes up on the bow, where she looks most dramatic in her bright dress. She tosses her black horsetail hair up and off one bare shoulder, then the other and squints into the sun, waving to incoming boats. To the larger boats, Roxanne waves and lifts her glass.

Sean and Bill, sailors by practice and Sean by build, are set about their tasks, all bicep and winch and line work. No one is at the helm. This happens every time they are leaving the marina. Bill runs around on deck, pulling up the main and Catherine sits there, nervously sipping her drink and battling the brim of the overzealous sun hat she must wear to keep from freckling and aging as fast as a banana. Before she ever sailed with him, Bill gave her a diagram of the boat and asked her to memorize it. "It just makes for better company when someone knows a jib from a cleat." Halyard, transom, backstay. A hard, weathered language. She knows every knot and screw. But, despite Bill's assurances, Catherine has no interest in steering her. She will only take the helm if there are rocks dead ahead. This has happened. And even then she just held her steady and hollered for Bill.

What wind there is, is a warm easterly wind, a Santa Ana, leaving the water flat, glassy. This is what Catherine hoped for in order to cook, though it also brings and settles the heat and smog of the valley onto the water—a thick orange light—and negates any actual sailing. Sean has removed his shirt. Bill wouldn't dare. The moon is visible, a white hook in the yellowed sky. The telltales snap and go slack against the sail.

Then, as they reach the mouth of the channel, the wind picks up just enough and the boat heels. Roxanne is tossed against a stanchion. Bill smiles. Catherine cuts the engine. Sean, audible now, is laughing. Roxanne retreats on all fours, clinging to the grabrail, her dress lifting up around her thighs.

"Assholes," she is saying. "Think you're so funny."

"We are men of many talents, Darling, but the winds we do not have our way with." Sean bends and gathers her up, like little more than a bundle of sticks. She wriggles, throwing elbows back against him. He bites her neck and she squeals. "Quiet down," he growls and wrestles her into the cockpit, across from Catherine. Catherine's hat has blown back. She fiddles with the cord at her throat, leaves the hat off. The sun is low enough. Sean wraps an arm around Roxanne and uses the other to maneuver her up onto his lap. It is a seamless motion, choreography they have executed before. "Bang, bang," he says. "Play dead." She goes limp against him—a game they've clearly played before. Roxanne's dress was wetted on one side; one breast, the hard pebble of her nipple is now visible, and her ribs. Sean rubs at her arm and legs. The flesh of her thigh goes from its olive tan to red with the force of his hand, the blood rising.

Catherine's husband, Thomas, had touched her like that. Practiced, firm, assured. He'd take her in his lap and hold her there, keep her in his arms so tight she had to close her eyes with the pleasure of it. Bill is more delicate, even careful with her. She is sure this has everything to do with her being a widow.

"Traveler, Bear," Bill says. This is all he says when he wants her to adjust the traveler, changing the angle of the mainsail. It's his abbreviation of Honey Bear, of course, but all she hears is the hulking weight of the word *Bear*. She adjusts the traveler, offering him a half-smile as she does.

She feels Roxanne watching her. Then Roxanne asks, "Why wasn't she steering?" tossing a hand in Catherine's direction.

Bill shrugs, "Why weren't you?"

Sean laughs.

"I'll get blankets," Catherine says. She can't help but catch sight again of the goose flesh on Roxanne's thighs, the hardened nipple of her wet breast. "It seems to be cooling off."

"And some food. I'm starved," Roxanne says.

"Of course."

The wake of a powerboat tosses Catherine around.

"Easy, Bear." Bill stops her lurching with a hand to her hip. A soft, gentle hand.

There are fishcakes, to be served chilled, and Bill made his horseradish dill sauce. The black morels and the radicchio are washed and ready. All that needs doing is the boiling of water for the penne and simmering the shrimp and vegetables with a pat of butter and dill. There isn't much of a gust, but Catherine has yet to cook, even on a glass-topped sea, without soiling or burning some article of clothing. Tonight must be different. She can cook on land. Quite well. Some of those meals have broken barriers before. Meals worth fawning over.

She raises up two blankets, offers a bowl of water crackers, crumbling slices of Pecorino in another bowl, and the bottle of vodka, which is passed and then handed back down empty. She fills the cooker, oils and salts the water.

"Look," Roxanne says above, "over there. A whole school of them."

"Pod," Bill corrects her.

Catherine has not seen dolphins here. In Hawaii with Thomas, yes, but not here. She takes one step up the companionway and sticks her head out. "Where?"

"Over there, just past that wave," Roxanne says. The ocean is somewhat choppy now, but no waves. Or is it all waves? Catherine eyes the shoreline and back, scanning left to right, as if reading the lines of a book. It's almost infuriating.

"Oh my," Sean says.

"Where?" Catherine asks.

"You missed it again? One just—right over there." Sean points to an area that seems a great expanse from where Roxanne had her eyes.

"Yep," Bill says, "Must be good fishing there. Happy little bunch."

"Little *pod,*" Roxanne says.

Catherine takes another step up and grazes her head on the boom. No one seems to notice. There is the woody smell of burning butter from down below.

"I want to dive right in and swim around with them." Roxanne wiggles against Sean.

Sean jerks her up, as if to toss her in. "Let me tie your ankles and hands first." This is how they talk to each other.

Boiling water spits and bubbles over down below. She hears it. Bill hears it, too.

"You've got pasta on?" he asks. "I can turn us in." He is offering to make things easier for her, to keep her from making a mess of herself, and the implication angers her; that her track record is so poor, that he smells something burning.

"I'm good," she says and ducks back down. There are no dolphins here.

As they were setting out, she pulled her hair back, as always, into a bun and Bill had taken the twisted knot of her hair in an inspective pinch of forefinger and thumb and muttered, "Like a little bale of hay." She's since let her hair down, but now, over the roll of the pasta and between her thoughts, she still hears the damn phrase. *Like a little bale of hay. Like a little bale of fucking hay.*

When she and Thomas learned that she was pregnant with James, Thomas said that with children comes the truth that you cannot reinvent yourself. "You are who you are. Children show you just who you are."

"I like who we are," she'd said.

"Nothing changes," he said. "We'll become our parents. We'll think we can be better than them, but we aren't." Thomas's parents were lacking. She watched him as he spoke, wondering where he was, his eyes on the ceiling. "We already are them, of course, but you really only have to face that if you have children."

This was just after the trip to Hawaii, where they had swum with the dolphins, when she was tan and felt beautiful and so pleased to be pregnant with his baby.

The radicchio is limp against the tongs. The mushrooms have bled brown into the noodles and the shrimp. But her shirt is clean. *You cannot reinvent yourself.* This phrase she also hears, between her thoughts, from time to time.

James has a father. *Has.* She'd said that to Bill earlier, hadn't she? Good wine does funny things with words and time.

Bill has dropped the mainsail and they are drifting. Catherine lifts each bowl up, one at a time. With the first offering, Sean moves Roxanne aside. He takes the bowl, sits with his legs open and eats. Roxanne crosses her arms. Catherine lifts another bowl and smiles to her. Catherine has found the making of women friends particularly hard here. Sean's mouth is shiny with oil. A 40-foot sloop slides by off the port side, the plastic dock fenders still dangling overboard.

"Beautiful," Sean says, his mouth full.

"Come on," Bill says. "How can you even see the damn boat when they don't pull their fenders in?"

"As bad as lawn ornaments," Catherine says.

"Lawn ornaments? So Midwest," Roxanne says this into Sean's shoulder, eyeing Catherine as if her shirt weren't clean. But Catherine said this, made this remark about the lawn ornaments, only because it was something she'd heard Bill say once. She hates this, too, her parroting. Roxanne is moving her fork around the bowl.

"So where are you from, Roxanne?" Catherine says now, sitting up straighter over her browned pasta.

"So tacky," Bill says, turning aft to follow the sloop away.

"Here," Roxanne says.

"Oh, please," Bill snorts. "You're from Temecula."

"Am not," Roxanne says.

"Yes you are," Sean says.

Her hand goes to Sean's thigh. "Can I tell them now?"

"Oh, right," Bill says, "your little story."

"It's not just a story," Roxanne pauses for some potential yet empty dramatic effect. "A murder," she says, her eyes tacking from Sean, to Bill, and settling on Catherine. "And a suicide."

"Anybody we know?" Bill says.

"You know that awful stucco colonial smash-up on the east side of our property?" Sean sweeps a finger down into his empty bowl.

"More?" Catherine offers.

Sean waves a no thanks and takes Roxanne's full bowl without missing a beat, then looks to Bill.

"The car collector?" Bill asks, eyes on the telltales.

"That's the one," Sean says.

"You're killing it, Sean. Let me," Roxanne says.

"These are your neighbors?" Catherine asks.

"Were our neighbors," Roxanne's eyes are beneath the shade of her angular hand. "He shot her in the bedroom upstairs." She says the word *shot* hard, with some pleasure. "Splattered her brains all over this awful Turkish rug and then offed himself in his BMW, all nice and neat." She wipes her hand across the air.

"He ruined that beautiful car," Bill says.

"No, no. He brought a hose from the exhaust in through the window. Textbook stuff," Sean says. "Literally, neatly."

"Were there children?" Catherine asks.

"No. But good question," Roxanne coos, pointing a flirtatious finger at Catherine. "The wife was a childless homemaker."

"I'll do the dishes," Catherine says, stupidly.

"Cath has a kid, Roxanne. A son, right?" Sean asks. "How old is he?"

"He's seven now," Catherine says. This isn't helping. She takes the two stacked bowls from Sean's lap, hoping not to speak about James any further.

"I'm thinking it was an affair," Roxanne is speaking to Bill. "Her affair. A pool boy kind of thing."

"A thing on the side is no reason to ruin an M5. They'll never get the stink of exhaust out of it, neat or not." Bill loves cars. Catherine has learned about cars, too.

Bill raises the mainsail. It billows and snaps, takes the wind, and the boat heels again. Catherine has to steady herself. Bill extends his bowl for collecting. She can't help but ignore him. She feels him pretending to pitch it overboard. She feels all of them laugh, silently, as she turns down the companionway stairs.

Down below everything slides toward her as she sets it down. She battles it back, then gives up, stacking everything in the sink.

Not one of them said anything about the meal. She suspects Sean would eat anything. Blood and gore. She can hear them talking above.

"You never heard them argue. Wasn't like that. But she could be a real pain. She's the one who gave us all the hell about the garage conversion last year. She had everyone signing petitions like it was going to block *all* of their views," Sean is saying.

"Mind your own yard, lady," Roxanne says.

Catherine brings up two bottles of Cabernet and the brick of dark chocolate.

"Oh, you're good," Bill says, nodding at her. "Just the thing."

She sits, keeping one bottle to herself.

"*I* wanted to kill her," Roxanne says and she seems to believe she is being funny.

"Was there a note left?" Catherine asks.

"As a matter of fact," Sean says. "My little Watson here,"—he has his hand on Roxanne's leg, under the blanket—"she managed to get a few details from a man in blue, didn't you, Wat?"

"Something Bass. That was his name. Like the fish. He wasn't supposed to tell me anything of course. But I, well, you—"

"You batted your eyes and etc., etc. Get on with it," Bill says, filling his plastic cup.

"*She was ruining me,*" Roxanne says, almost hissing. "That's what he told me. Bass. That's what the note said. *She was ruining me.*"

"That's it?" Bill asks.

"Well, there was more, I'm sure. But that's the juicy bit."

"That could be financial. Doesn't have to be an affair. Ruining someone."

"Or maybe the *she,*" Sean says, edgy with an epiphany, "wasn't his wife at all."

A dolphin pierces the water off the starboard side. A bed of red kelp slips past.

"Catherine, are you crying?" Roxanne asks.

"No. I don't think so. No." Her mouth is wet *and* dry with the red wine. How does it do that?

"Catherine lost a husband to cancer." Bill gives his most earnest nod. Hollow as a ship.

"I'm sorry," Sean says. "This is your son's father? Is that right? How awful."

Another dolphin breaks and drops. Like a needle through fabric, up and back down. A stitch in time. That fucking saying. Thomas had wanted to go to India, Africa. Hawaii was just simple, starter travel. They'd talked about Cambodia. The trip to South America: it was planned, mapped, booked, but the morning sickness had set in and the doctor made her nervous about the drinking water, about having adequate nutrition. Thomas was too good to travel without her.

"It wasn't cancer, " Catherine says. "Thomas. My husband. He was the healthiest man I've ever met. Except for you Sean, of course. You're very virile. Clearly. But Thomas, he ran five miles every morning. No matter the weather. Five miles every morning. Sometimes ten." Roxanne reaches across Catherine. The still-damp fabric of her dress grazes Catherine's arm. It stops her. "Bill," Catherine says, "hand Roxanne that bottle already."

The bottle is passed. Bill gets to his feet. He is pulling the mainsail up. Catherine feels his eyes on her, a sideways glance. "We're going to come about," he says, readying them to tack the boat.

Catherine does not look up again. They want a story. She lets her eyes close. "On the hottest days, at the end of a run, Thomas would jog right into the house and strip down. He'd drop his shorts and shirt and ring them out under the faucet of our pantry." Catherine is there, in the kitchen, watching him. "He'd take them to the line we'd strung from the back of the house out to the garage and he would leave his clothes hanging there, the weight of them slung against the line." The line from the house out to the garage. The line. When Bill had given her the diagram of the boat, after she said she'd memorized it, he asked her to close her eyes and walk through the boat, to tell him the parts of the boat. It was the most attracted she ever was to Bill. Rope. She kept saying rope, when she knew it was called a line. The rope from the house out to the garage. She closes her eyes in the garage. "Thomas hung himself in our garage. My husband."

Bill says something, but she cannot make it out. She adjusts the traveler, just in case, smiling at the sound of it tightening. There is satisfaction in that sound, everything becoming taut. But it wasn't summer then, of course. It was nearly the dead of winter. And Thomas had stopped jogging months before. But that's who Thomas was. He was someone who jogged, no matter the weather.

"'Maybe if you run,' I said to him. 'If you just start running again. You'll feel better.' But he stopped wanting to. I don't even know if the clothesline was up anymore. But that's what he used." She can see past Sean and Roxanne, to the shore, yet still make out their faces, their empty gazes, or maybe that is pity. "Not cancer. It wasn't that simple," she says. To be clear. She wants to be clear: it wasn't that bad. Nothing so long and drawn out as cancer.

Sean asks if Bill is okay. Of course, he is. Bill is always okay. "That pasta was really, just, tremendous," Sean says, going on about the horrid sauce.

She feels the boat give and lift. She understands: Bill is bringing them back in. He has sat down beside her. She feels his grip on her leg. Firm. Not the usual Bill. Damn it, Catherine, there's no rope on a boat. She had had to scold herself. Bow line. Stern line. Spring line. Her hand has come to rest at her collarbone, the slipped noose of her own hand. How embarrassing she is. Bill could take her and lift her up right now—flip her up and over, into the water. Maybe tie her feet and hands first. The shock of the cold water. How perfect that would be. But Bill would never do that.

Bill will say, only after they are home, *You told me he was sick*. Catherine will be defensive, sour, an old hurt burrowing in her chest. He was sick! *Obviously*, she will say. Who does such a thing? And then Bill will call James into the room, tell him to sit down, and proceed to say something stiff and uncomfortable. Like, *I understand you better now, son*. But there is nothing to understand. Sometimes Catherine can hear James's thoughts. Her son's simple, pleading thoughts.

Bill is talking to Roxanne in that clipped familiar tone.

"It was just a story," Roxanne is saying.

"I wasn't steering the boat," Catherine says, "because of the wind. It doesn't matter how much you know about a boat." A cormorant submerges and bobs back, choking a fish down its fleshy gullet. Only the water, the birds—nothing else moves. "Bill," Catherine says, an ache has moved in to her throat. No one speaks.

"The wind goes one way and then it just shifts." She strikes the metal of the boom. Roxanne startles. "Bam."

"It's okay," Bill says. "We'll be in by dark."

It is Sean who hands Catherine another drink.

Bill is telling a joke about sailors. He has stood up, his short square frame at the helm, the shot of mast before him, his back is to her. It was raining that night. Nothing else had been different. By morning, the driveway was skinned with ice an inch thick. How careful Thomas must have been, walking out to the garage. A wide, sturdy, purposeful gait, like sea legs. But Catherine is here now, off the coast of California, wedged into the laughter of half-familiar people, all of them having moved on. The shore dips and rises, the blunt line of apartment buildings there, the windows catching the last rusty light of the setting sun, glinting like pennies in a shallow wishing well.

Man Down Below

Eddie says, "Do you want to know what I think?" And you think, *No, dear god, not Eddie.*

You are standing at the newsstand, one block from your new apartment, and you have to wonder if he saw you, if he saw you walk from your front door down to this corner and if he is going to be right here tomorrow, holding out a cup of coffee, waiting for you. "What do you think, Eddie?" you ask, turning around. No, there is no getting rid of him once he's spotted you.

"I think you've been avoiding me," he says.

"I'm sorry you feel that way," you say. Not apologizing, but accepting a true and accurate fact.

"Have you been avoiding me?"

"I've been living."

"What the hell does that mean?" he says, without altering his voice, no sign of anger. Shouldn't the word *hell* call for some inflection?

"It means I've been living my life and I've not given any thought to avoiding you. I just haven't seen you. And, well, here you are!"

In your last apartment, Eddie lived below you. He knew when you were home, when you showered, what you cooked for dinner, what shows you watched, and when you had a lover—that was when you had to move. That was only a month ago. You *have* been avoiding him.

"You didn't tell me you were moving. You must have done it while I was at work. I never saw a moving van. Not until the new tenant. Her name's Rebecca, too."

"Her name's Rebecca, huh?" you ask, wondering if this is true or if Eddie has just totally flipped, if he was as obsessed with you as you thought he was in your very worst of nightmares. And yes, you moved while he was at work. He works a nightshift at some bizarre, dimly-lit—you think porn-stockpiled—video store. It's open all night for fuck's sake! You had to pay the movers extra and get special permission from the supers in both buildings. You weren't surprised when they didn't ask why. They're just supers. They don't care until someone complains and people in this part of town don't do that, the housing situation being too precarious, too cutthroat. It's one of the reasons you like this city, everything is a little harder than necessary—it weeds out the weaklings. Like Eddie, you'd think. But Eddie is still hanging on and you wonder, looking at him now, if you have underestimated him. He found you, no problem. "That's convenient," you tell him. "No need for me. I've been accurately replaced."

"This Rebecca's a cross-dresser," Eddie says, matter of fact. "His real name is Frank. He's Rebecca Monday through Friday."

"Good for her, for him," you say, folding your newspaper and clamping it between your elbow and side.

Eddie is no dummy. He senses you readying yourself for an all out sprint up the hill, back to your new apartment, back to shelter. It is only seven A.M. and you are already exhausted. Eddie has exhausted you.

"Don't go," he says, pushing his hands, palms down, against the air, like he's telling a dog to stay. I'm no fucking dog, you think. You can't urge me to stay, but your feet aren't moving. He has big hands. You hadn't noticed before.

"Just tell me why you moved?" he pleads.

You start to wonder if honesty really is the best policy or if a well-groomed tale might entertain him to some point of satisfaction. But you can't think fast enough and suddenly the truth is standing tall on your tongue, arm crooked in a proud pose of damn-it-I'm-right-here, use me!

"I moved because of you."

He doesn't look hurt or anything. He looks like he was expecting this and suddenly you realize he's getting off on it. Not a hard-on, but he's enjoying it, like you're performing some relationship breakup scene played out far too often on just this kind of street corner. He is absorbing, harnessing the power of the effect that he has had on you—his power over you. Now you're supposed to say something like, "No, no, it wasn't you. It's me. I have to figure some things out. I just need time." Did you really say that? Your free hand goes to your face, concealing the tremor of a laugh threatening to escape. "I'm sorry," you say. But now he does look hurt. You've broken the moment, forgotten your line, this scene is a wrap. Will he cry?

"I didn't mean to frighten you," he says. The words sound broken up with spittle, but he remains calm, his eyes appear only moist, maybe yearning. Hungry is the word. "I just like you," he says, eyes dead-on, on you.

This is working. He's getting to you. Don't let him get to you.

"You didn't frighten me, Eddie. I just need more privacy. For my work." You write restaurant reviews and two separate cooking columns for the free rags. You are at this newsstand to review your bit on high-fat diets. You're all for them. This is your bit—it's what you get for a bachelor's in English and a short stint in culinary school. It's all you get. And you don't need privacy, but just the opposite, you need lots of *things*. Things to keep you from that rattling panic, always ready to encroach with your next glance at the clock, the realization you have nowhere to be. You have to be nowhere. Nowhere is great. You can totally hang with nowhere.

The truth is—you shy from admitting it—but in the quiet afternoons, when normal people are at their offices, Eddie was the most perfect distraction for you. He made you feel interesting, you were so interesting, and he—he was the freak. But you don't live there, above Eddie, anymore, do you? He is not the man down below anymore, is he?

"Was I really so bad?" he asks.

You've never made eye contact with Eddie before now, not like this. Locked. You remember the time he came up, knocking just as you were getting out of the shower. He'd heard the water and he must have heard the grunts and chirps of sex before that. It was intentional. You could tell. He wanted Mario to come to the door—Mario, your half Spanish lover, the waiter from Casa Don Antonio's, since gone into the oblivion of all old lovers (an oblivion as though you'd returned them to the store that they came from, as though they'd never walked the same streets or sat at the same bar stools that they had when you found them and brought them home—this city is so big, the sprawl and all that). Eddie needed that detail, needed to see the face of the man who'd just been inside you, just as before he'd needed the details of your cooking. He'd call to ask what spice that was in the spaghetti sauce, the curry, the salmon, even the macaroni and cheese—the man has the snout of a bloodhound.

Suddenly this weight in your mind—the images of Eddie in his dimly lit apartment, everything a different shade of gray, the buzz of traffic, the idea that you moved to have lovers and now you wonder why you call them lovers when you never ever love them, the sight of Eddie before you, his hurt—the weight of it all falls to your hands and you reach up and out to touch Eddie. It is a moment you see at some distance, a home movie of you, there, reaching for Eddie, pulling his body to yours. You are so removed you don't yet feel it. You are watching Rebecca. You, Rebecca, are hugging Eddie, the slightly greasy guy from downstairs, and you seem to be enjoying it right up until now. He has the odor of mushrooms. How is that possible? How can someone smell like mushrooms? And you're back, back in your shoes, back on the corner, outside the newsstand, holding icky Eddie from downstairs, in his—is that a raincoat? In his raincoat that does indeed smell of mushrooms. What is under that raincoat? It *never* rains.

You step back. One step, two. You are walking backwards into traffic. There are horns, the sound of brakes and tires.

"Was I really so bad?" he says, again, above the traffic. His arms are still parentheses of the broken embrace.

"You were fine," you mouth, pushing breath up, but nothing sounds out. "You did fine," you try again, getting only the "You" to appear. He starts after you. Not in a hurry, but as though you had invited him for a walk.

You turn around to pick up speed, to push from your toes. You feel him behind you. You drop the paper and start pulling at the air with your clenched hands. You are running up this hill. You don't look back. You are totally out of shape.

In your new apartment, you lock and double-check the lock and pull the blinds down.

You look at your phone. Nothing flashing, no light. No one has called.

You lean your head against the window, then peek below the blinds, out with one eye. Eddie is not waiting outside. Eddie is not living beneath you. He is going home, to be beneath the new Rebecca. You wonder what she dresses like. If the wig is brown, curly, red, straight. You have dirt-brown hair. Shoulder length, without style. It is your most average of so many average features.

You imagine walking over to the old building and standing outside, waiting to see the new Rebecca, see if she goes to a day job, Monday through Friday. If she wears pumps and a suit. You think you could write an article for the weekly—Transvestites Working It. Then cut the "It." Then put it back. You smile at the idea of going to spy on the Rebecca that lives above Eddie. Oh, no, the irony is not lost on you. You wonder if Eddie calls him, her, if he knocks at the door nightly. Which voice does Rebecca use to answer the phone? Does she clear her throat before lifting her chin, tightening up into a squeak of a voice? *Becca here.*

You decide Eddie has gone and it is okay to open the blinds. Light, you get good southern light in the morning—warming the room and your overall feeling. You touch your toes, stretch out the run fatigue that is settling into your thighs. Stretching is good. Why don't you do this more often? You think of your cat (horrified that you are a woman with a cat who thinks of having plural cats!), and how your cat is always stretching, rolling over in the sun, letting it fall on her belly. You take off your shirt, undo your bra, and lower yourself to the floor, loosening your jeans. You are not alone. You have a cat.

The sun does not feel as warm as your cat makes it look. The bare floor is rather cold. You wish you were covered in fur, that your nails were so long you could sink their sharpened little ends into anything and everything, ruining things. You roll over onto all fours and arch your back. You took an acting class once—to meet men. The instructor said *Be an animal. Make like a wild beast. Howl, cackle, koo-koo till you are blue in the face.* And you did. You did.

When you stand up and open the blinds, Eddie is outside the window. He is holding two cups of coffee. You have two exposed breasts. You animal. Eddie does not look away. You hiss and lash at the air, your fingers curled like claws, ready to latch on. Eddie knows you take two sugars, one cream.

Blue

The widow was demonstrating how to feed the dog by dipping a cup into the bag of kibble, bringing it up empty, then putting a can of wet food on the counter and moving the can opener around it like a pantomime, before finally circling the empty bowl with a spoon—all of this as if Josie were stone dumb, never mind the torture this pretend feeding was on the poor dog, Blue. Josie could hear him behind her in the doorway: his wet breathing and the slap of his tongue to teeth, his provoked hunger. He was some kind of longhaired, gray mutt. When Josie left for college, less than a year ago, the widow had not owned a dog. But here he was now looking as old as the widow, only slightly more upright. The widow let the spoon clatter in the metal bowl, saying, "Not too much, not too little," lifting one finger up to some god of knowledge. The gesture reminded Josie of her college professors. Josie hadn't liked being told what to think and that's all college seemed to be about, however sideways they came at it.

Blue barked once, a raspy impatient bark. The widow turned and scolded him with her eyes, then opened the backdoor to the thin strip of yard. Blue reluctantly lumbered outside, turning around to face them as the door closed.

"He'll need to be walked," the widow said. "Not just left in the yard. Not everyone's gonna shit where they eat." The widow always spoke this way, leaving Josie insulted, though she was never sure an insult was intended.

"Walk the dog," Josie said. "Got it." Josie had agreed to watch the widow's house and the dog for the month of July and into August, while the widow traveled. There wasn't any money in it, but Josie was glad to be out of her mother's house for a while, and maybe, Josie reasoned, Tim Gibbons would spend the night with her there.

"So where are you going?" Josie asked.

The widow was picking up small pictures and little china figurines off of the tables and mantel, then setting them inside a cabinet, as if to protect them from Josie. "I have six children," the widow said.

For a time, the widow had had cats and there was a bright white bird kept in a cage at the living-room window, but in the ten years that Josie and her mother lived next door to the widow, Josie never saw any children, grown or otherwise. The size of the widow's house made more sense now. It was as dilapidated a house as Josie's mother's, but it had multiple floors and the windows were bigger and more frequent, and that made it seem better somehow, more desirable, even if it was just a larger mess. But that these rooms had once held children, years ago, before Josie was even a thought—the quiet in this house, Josie understood, must be that much larger too.

The widow was still setting away pictures. "Six. Wow. I didn't know." Josie said.

Josie was an only child. Her father was long gone, though her mother had been married to Hank for a time. Josie had liked Hank. He had kept horses and taught her to ride. Since he'd left,

Josie had gotten used to a certain amount of quiet—a quiet that college had disrupted. She had still not told her mother, Miriam, that she wasn't just home for the summer, that she had in fact dropped out altogether.

"It seems neither do they. Promises are easily made. So I'm going to them. Hurrying, before I keel over. Michigan, Kansas, Houston. My youngest in Houston can help with the driving."

"You're driving?" The only car in front of the widow's house was the same Chrysler sedan as always, more yellowed than painted yellow. Josie had been tempted to kick at the side panel when she'd come up the drive, see if it gave. "I'm dating this mechanic. I mean, if you wanted him to take a look before you go."

"A mechanic? Yes, I'm sure you are. There's no time for that."

Outside, Blue was staring at a squirrel balanced on the phone wire. The squirrel frozen still—a practiced stillness, an attempt at invisibility. "How old is Blue?" Josie asked. "You just get him? You had that white bird when I left."

"You left?"

"Yes, college."

Josie thought she'd feel at home, dropping out and coming back, but she felt just the opposite. It was as if the house, her mother, even this dog of the widow's were all part of a slightly off replacement of the life she thought she'd been living. College was confusing, even disconcerting, but wasn't that expected? Her boxes unpacked, she was considering this, she knew, too late.

"Well, that bird," the widow said. "The cage, the seed, the feces. The squawking! The dog is new. And, yes, old."

Josie was looking at the yellow sedan again, worrying for the widow, feeling that someone should.

Josie had started seeing Tim Gibbons the same week she came back home. He was fixing up the truck that Hank—her stepfather, ex-stepfather—had left behind. Josie thought about Tim often, but anxiously, like an obligation, a test for which she had yet to prepare. Tim had an apartment that he shared with another mechanic. The place had the sour odor of feet.

The widow was touching a piece of paper on the mantel. "These are the numbers you'll need. My children. The veterinarian."

"There won't be any problems," Josie said.

"Of course not," the widow said. "You promise, I'm sure."

For the first few days Josie stayed at the widow's house she left the television on whether she was watching or not. She sat outside in her underwear, in the sunshine, eating bowl after bowl of cereal and drinking from the juice carton. The dog followed behind her every step and he was, after all, perfectly happy to shit in the small rectangular yard. The widow said Josie could help herself to the pantry *and whatnot,* but had insisted she sleep in one of the downstairs bedrooms.

When Josie came back inside, when the sun had begun its descent, Josie took naps, often lying down before her eyes even adjusted to the dim interior of the house, feeling full and light all at once, waking when it was near dark and then remaining up for half the night. She had quickly found a level of contentment with doing nothing for which she knew she ought to feel guilty. From the bedroom she'd chosen she could see the dirt turnaround in front of her mother's house and so she knew which of her mother's boyfriends was there to visit, when.

The guy who came in the first half of the week was the married one. Brian or Rick or Dave. Josie had talked to him only once, but she preferred him to the other one because he was married and therefore quiet, neat, and polite. He drove an American car, a Chrysler LeBaron, white with a moon roof, and he always left before dusk, usually straightening his tie.

The second guy was an operating room nurse and he rode a Japanese motorcycle. He stayed for entire weekends, drinking every last drop of beer and eating anything Miriam hadn't hidden. Miriam joked that the first half of her week—Rick, Brian, Dave, whatever—paid for the second half. Josie didn't put it past her mother to be extorting a married man. In fact, if she was, Josie applauded her—in part for the wife. But this other guy, this nurse, left Josie in disbelief. The gluttonous, sloppy owner of a Honda motorcycle who spoke to her mother as if she were just another piece of household technology that he found frustrating to operate.

Tim Gibbons worked on American cars.

By Thursday, rations had thinned at the widow's, and Josie went down to her mother's, knowing the nurse was there. Miriam was in the kitchen, washing dishes by hand—given the state of the dishwasher. Before agreeing to dogsit, Josie had made a list of the things that needed fixing around her mother's house. She was planning on fixing them, to make herself useful, before she mentioned that bit about dropping out.

"You steal from her yet?" Miriam asked, tossing her head in the direction of the widow's.

Josie slid into the kitchen booth, avoiding the end where the vinyl had begun to crack. "Not yet," she said. "What's for dinner?"

The nurse walked in and handed Miriam a plate. "What's she doing here?"

"I live here, Eric," Josie said. The nurse's name was Stan, but Josie called him any name except his own, usually names of Miriam's former boyfriends. Except Hank. She never called him Hank.

Stan rolled his eyes. He was short, with the body of a gnome, packed into his pit-stained nursing scrubs. Josie found him equal parts comical and offensive. He pulled out a beer and twisted it open. "Miriam," he said, wiping his mouth, "I thought we had the place to ourselves."

"We've already eaten, Josie. You'll have to fix yourself something."

"You ought to make her pay for the food," Stan said, moving back into the living room, settling into the big chair, into the groove where Hank had liked to sit.

"He's the one who should pay." Josie lowered her voice—asking through her teeth, "Why do you put up with him?"

"I like him," Miriam said. She had turned around, leaning against the sink and toweling off the plate, but she didn't look up at Josie. "Honestly, Josie, it isn't your concern."

Josie caught sight of the car headlights just before they swept through the kitchen, whipping around the dirt turnaround. Tim Gibbons didn't have his own car, so Josie never knew when she'd see him, when he'd pick her up. He drove the cars he was working on. Tonight he had a red Chevy. He stopped, the engine running. He wasn't going to get out or come in. Things weren't like that.

"I'm going out," Josie said.

She started for the door, then stopped to look in the long mirror, where other people might keep a coat rack, something sensible, but this was Los Angeles: you needed a mirror, not a coat.

She could see Stan behind her in the mirror, his back to her, the television lit up and spitting basketball plays.

"You're fucking kidding me," Stan shouted, slamming his beer up then down, letting it slosh out.

Josie jumped. She could feel her mother watching her. Tim honked. "I have to go," she said.

"Who's stopping you?" Stan said over his shoulder.

Josie turned to Miriam, to find her eyes, to see if she was going to let him talk to her like this. Miriam looked back at her, but said nothing.

"Really?" Josie asked.

Miriam set the dried plate on the counter and began to towel another. Before going, Josie opened a button on her shirt, exposing the slope of her breasts.

Josie hadn't known Tim was coming, but she'd been hoping, and then there he was, like an epiphany—a relief. Blue was barking above, behind the widow's fence.

The handle was missing on the outside of the passenger door; Josie reached for it twice before Tim leaned across the seat. "You gonna fix that?" she said, getting in. "You're a mechanic, right?"

"Girls like it when a guy opens the door."

His cigarette was teetering on the lip of the ashtray, stringing smoke through the car. Josie took a drag, then handed it back, saying, "different girl."

Tim studied the cigarette. "Nasty," he said. He swerved left.

"Would you slow down?"

"It's not a pacifier. You don't have to put your tongue on it." He lit a new cigarette off the old one, steering the car with his knee.

Their go-to discussion was always whether or not Tim had any memory of her in high school. He said he'd found his senior yearbook yesterday, where she was a freshman. "I do remember you in high school," he said. "You were cuter than I remembered, though."

"Dill used to spit on my lunch tray." Dill was Tim's best friend, then and now. Josie wondered why she wasn't this way, why she'd never hung on to friends. She always felt a little bit liquid. Her full name was Josie Post, a name from a father of whom she had no memory. Dill had turned her name into a tag line for just about anything he felt the need to mock: *ain't that as dumb as a Josie Post.*

"You've blossomed. What can I say?" Tim had his hand on her thigh, kneading the muscle above her knee. The first time he'd grabbed her like this she'd yelped, but now she didn't mind. She practiced relaxing toward the pain.

Tim would never have noticed her return home—let alone her—if she hadn't had Hank's truck towed into the shop where he worked. The truck had been sitting under a tarp for years. From the reception area she saw Tim slide out from under a Buick, oil running down his arm like a long black glove. She asked the receptionist if he could be the one to give her the estimate. "Whatever," the woman said, smacking her gum, and called Tim over. Josie had recognized him. She remembered him, of course. He was familiar, something unchanged. And dating him, that he'd taken an interest in her immediately, made her feel she wasn't so wrong to have come home. Six weeks later and Hank's truck was still sitting in the back of the auto shop. They didn't talk about it, but Josie felt that the truck's still not being fixed somehow defined their present and future, like something of a promise ring.

If he ever fixed it, they were over.

Tim pulled off at the lookout, as usual. Josie opened the glove box to find the bottle of Jim Beam he stashed in whichever car he took. She uncapped it and slipped her shoes off and cranked the seat low enough so that all she could see were the two or three stars visible behind the screen of smog. Josie had wanted to leave L.A. so badly, get as far as she could, filling out only out-of-state applications, but here she was all over again. The whiskey warmed her: down her throat, inside her chest, moving through her until the whisper of its heat rested between her legs. The first few swallows always did this, but if he didn't touch her soon enough she grew irritable, solitary. She put her feet up on the dash and tapped her toes to the glass, pinning the stars.

"Kiss my ankles," she said to Tim. "Then my calves, my wrists, then this dip in my arm." She mapped a finger over the blue vein that ran from her wrist clear along the line of her bicep. "How am I still pale?" she said, almost laughing—riding that first quick dip toward drunk.

Tim hadn't moved toward her. She looked at him. His lips shone wet with the whiskey. His hands and face were always a little bit dirty.

"Look, there's a fire," he said, squinting one eye. "I think it's that clapboard house next to school."

Josie remembered hearing rumors about Tim and Dill shooting up rats in the clapboard. She knew Tim didn't remember her from high school. "Good," Josie said, closing her eyes. "Maybe the whole school will catch."

While Tim fucked her, Josie made moans of encouragement, but he'd waited too long and she kept thinking of the list of things that needed fixing in her mother's house. The vinyl in the kitchen booth. The dishwasher was the most irritating; scrubbing dishes while right there stood that useless hunk of plumbing. Josie adjusted her hips to shift some of Tim's pressure—he wasn't so drunk. She bit down on his shoulder. There were the mini blinds, too, in her mother's room. They'd been bent in half somehow—a somehow Josie didn't really want to consider. They needed replacing.

There was little different about her mother after Hank left. A veneer hardened, maybe, gone matte. Josie had wanted to be away from all her stiff silences, but then once gone, she found herself turning around in her mind, looking back home, thinking about her mother in particular, about her being alone, missing her. But Miriam wasn't alone at all. Miriam was never alone.

Tim arched his back and Josie saw the hairs of his nose quiver with his exhale. What was Josie doing with herself, here, watching the widow's dog? There was a fist in her belly, an ache. Tim moved from her, back behind the steering wheel. Then he thanked her, as he always did.

"For what?" she said, this time.

He reached for his shirt. "I dunno. Just seems like I should."

The dog woke Josie, looking at her like he knew something, like an earthquake was coming. Josie fed him, but he wouldn't eat, whimpering and circling, making Josie uneasy. The TV was still on. It was a drought year, like all the rest, but the fire at the clapboard house had not spread. It took only one fire truck and two men half-heartedly arching water into its center to put it out. Josie went down to her mother's to tell her about the fire, Blue following behind, shadowing her as he did now.

Miriam made her breakfast. "Why's that dog smell wet?" she asked.

"He's being weird. You want him outside?" Josie offered. Stan was still asleep, upstairs.

"No, it's fine. Kinda nice to have a dog in the house again," she said. Hank had taken their dog when he left: injury to insult. "Too bad the school didn't catch," Miriam said, surprising Josie.

Some days this happened. Some days they could fall back toward one another, when there was room for them to do so. Maybe this was what Josie was back for, for these moments when Miriam looked at her and they both said I'm sorry and I forgive you and I love you with only their eyes and maybe half a smile, and Josie felt seen. They finished their eggs and sat, Miriam sipping coffee. It was growing hot already.

"You want my car?" Miriam said. "For the day? If you want to get out for a while."

In this, her mother's contented company, the uneasiness Josie had woken with turned to a giddy kind of bravery. She would go and see Tim at the shop, unexpectedly, unannounced—the way he came to her.

Halfway out the door, Josie stopped. "I can fix the dishwasher when I get back."

"Leave it to Stan," Miriam said, "it's the least he can do."

When Josie pulled up, Tim was sitting in a car outside the shop, a Honda—of all the cars. There was a girl, a redhead, in the driver's seat.

Tim was kissing her.

First, Josie's breath deepened, her heart slowed, a primal reaction: flight or fight. But then a quiet vindication moved in. Josie knew this already—an expectation was being met, a primitive script enacted. This was the same kind of understanding she'd had away at school, an awareness of the futility underneath the brick and ivy, the desks. This, she knew, was the kind of wisdom that went hand in hand with a certain sadness. Finally, she leaned on the horn of her mother's car. In the backseat, Blue started barking.

Two mechanics came out, looking around, in their coveralls. Tim jumped out of the Honda and waved at Josie, smiling, earnest as ever. He waved off the other mechanics to go on about their business. Then he leaned down, into the open window of the Honda and said something to the redheaded girl, something that made that girl smile a big rabbit-toothed smile before she drove off, waving in Josie's direction.

"She's my cousin," Tim said.

"You kiss your cousin?" After the girl had gone, Josie got out of her mother's car, leaned against it, her arms crossed. Blue was panting in the backseat, watching them.

"Her cheek, Josie. We're close." He put his hands on Josie's hips and wiggled her, as if they might dance.

"You were all over her," Josie said.

She knew better than to believe him and she told him so. She pushed his hands away. She got back into her mother's car, slamming the door, and drove away with Blue barking out the window.

Her cheeks were flush. Her foot and knee began shaking against the gas pedal. She was, possibly, more exhilarated by acting jealous than she was actually jealous. His cousin was pretty, in a peculiar way. In the kind of way girls at school had been, comfortable and confident, despite a pimple, despite tangled hair, and unafraid when Josie looked at them a little too long. Toward the end of the year, at a party, after Josie had already failed to secure her loans or register for new classes, a girl had leaned over and kissed Josie on the mouth. Josie had, briefly, kissed back. There was nothing quiet about college.

When Josie returned the car, Stan's motorcycle was gone. Inside, the dishwasher was open and its door was halfway dismantled from its frame, a crescent wrench left on the counter. Josie called for Miriam though she could tell her mother wasn't there, that she was somewhere on the back of that motorcycle, her arms around Stan.

The widow's house was bigger, quieter, and that much more empty, too.

Blue looked at Josie.

"What now?" she asked him. His tail thumped the floor.

Josie looked at the classifieds and ate soup crackers for a while, then brushed herself off and went to the cabinet where the widow had tucked away most of the frames and figurines. She set a few of the photos back out. These were, Josie realized, the widow's grown children, with their own children, no longer feeling the pull of this house on them, if they ever felt it at all. On the mantel, alongside the list of telephone numbers, Josie found a road map. Surely the widow had another. Josie spread it open on the coffee table, driving a finger over the threading of highways, finding Houston—where the widow might be—then to Wyoming, looking for the dot of the town where she knew Hank had moved.

Blue didn't bark when Tim came up the road, but stayed asleep, having finally eaten his well-mixed food. Tim was in one of the shop's trucks this time. She had told him about the widow's place the night before, at the lookout, before she'd known about the other girl. But Josie was too bored to stay mad or to pretend to stay mad, so she went to the mailbox at the end of the widow's driveway, collecting the mail she hadn't been collecting. Tim unzipped his blue coveralls and tugged on jeans before circling a clean white tee over his head, swinging his hips. "You home all alone, little girl?"

Tim was ropey thin, with a mop of brown hair. Josie was never sure if she wanted to touch him or laugh at him. She kicked at the dust of the road and averted her eyes, playing along. She liked that he was here, that he was here instead of with the redheaded girl. Tim grabbed her by the hips and walked her backwards through the door, saying, "You ain't mad at me," without any hint of it being a question.

Josie shrugged. What had made that other girl laugh?

"Jesus," he said, "old people's places give me the creeps." He sat down on the couch and lifted up the afghan, peering under as though something dead might be beneath. "Stinks like oatmeal in here."

She sat down across from him. "It's better than your place." She folded up the map on the table.

"What are you doing way over there? Come sit on grandpa's lap."

"So, we're family now, too?" She was smirking, but got up and moved over beside him. "This house makes me kind of sad."

Before the widow had demonstrated feeding the dog, she had taken Josie down the hall, toward the master bedroom, but then stopped short of opening the door, as if just remembering something. "I'd prefer you sleep in one of the spare rooms," she said. "I won't have time to tidy up in here and the linens are clean in all the other rooms." Then the widow's tone turned stern. "I insist you stay in another room." This was fine with Josie. She hadn't had her heart set on sleeping in some old lady's bed. She'd looked in all the spare rooms, the grown children's rooms, before choosing the only one with the queen bed and the view to the driveway below.

She touched the curl of hair behind Tim's ear, then rested her head on his shoulder, inhaling the burnt scent of him. Blue waddled in, sniffing his boots.

"There's that dog," Tim said. "Not barking at me now, are you, mutt?"

Josie heard Stan's motorcycle returning down below. She listened for her mother's voice, if she could hear them talking, laughing. Nothing. "His name is Blue," Josie said.

"Bluesy-woozy," Tim said, taking the dog's head in his hands and rattling it back and forth. Josie closed one eye and slouched down, making it look like Tim was wearing the lampshade from the lamp across the room.

"What are you doing?"

"Giving you a hat." That girl, the redhead, her smile; she hadn't cared who Josie was at all.

"You're a strange one, Josie Post."

"Am I?" Josie smiled, then moved her hand from his thigh, up to the button fly of his jeans, fingering the lip of fabric, the cool metal of the buttons. When she first arrived at college, a slumped-nosed woman in the registrars' office had asked, as if reading the question off a grocery list, "Who do you want to be?" The woman's dispassionate cadence, the way she seemed to wait for a response as if there were only wrong answers; Josie had only shrugged. That girl, Josie thought now.

Tim stood and took her by the hand. "Let's do it on the old lady's bed."

She led him around the corner, down the hall, stopping at the same door where the widow had stopped, and leaned against it, letting him rub between her legs until she was suffering the seam of her shorts hard against her pelvic bone. She felt for the doorknob behind her, twisting and pushing until they fell inside.

The room was enormous and unusually bright, the openness of the space, the blank white palette—they were quickly distracted from one another. Tim moved to the armoire, flipping open a polished silver box, smashing down the bristles on a horsehair brush. This was, by far, the largest room in the house. It was as if the widow had walls knocked down and built a sanctuary. Josie understood why she had not brought her in, proud of it, but more protective in the end. The room was very clean. The dog wandered in, smelling the carpet as if he'd never been inside. Tim lit a cigarette.

"I don't think we should smoke in here," Josie said. The dog seemed to hear something and ran from the room. Josie heard the crack of the back door hitting the brick she'd propped it open on.

Tim sat on the bed. He ran his hand over the twisted wrought iron of the bed's frame. "We shouldn't be in here at all," he said. "But this," he blew smoke toward Josie's face, "would be the perfect place to tie you up. Make you bark." He made a snarling face, his lip curling up, exposing his teeth.

Josie laughed a high, nervous laugh and turned away from him, moving toward the window. She stood there, feeling him behind her. All the muscles, the skin of her back, the fine hairs at her neck, aware of him, so much so that she did not yet see beyond the yard. First she watched Blue—he was poised beneath the phone line, another squirrel clinging to a phone wire above, trying desperately to be still, to wait Blue out. All animals, Josie thought, must know this waiting, how to steady the breath, stiffen, one anticipating the chance to have the other. And then there she was. Above the low, thin tines of the widow's flaking red fence—there was Miriam, her mother, behind the broken mini blinds of her bedroom, bent as they were, like a set of white metal wings, turned at just such an angle that, from here, Josie could see in, see her mother and Stan—clear enough.

Josie turned away, feeling the pressure of Tim's fingers curling against the bone of her hip. He was always grabbing her fucking hips.

"What are you looking at?" he asked, and pulled the lace of the widow's curtain back more. "Fuck," he said. "Is that your mom?"

"Stop looking," Josie said. She touched his shoulder, wanting to turn him back to her, but she felt the determination, the weight of his lean toward the window. She took the cigarette from him. She drew the smoke into her mouth, felt the burn of it and let the curling lip of ash fall to the carpet. She sat on the bed. What, she thought, was lost in him seeing? "Please, stop looking," she said, again.

"You jealous?" he asked.

"I'm bored," she said. The cigarette was a nub of fire. She considered pressing it into her palm, building a well of singed flesh in the middle of her hand.

"He's got her—" Tim started. "Fuck. He is rough." Tim was quiet for a minute, watching, then he said, "Josie," just her name, and then, finally, almost asking, but not: "She likes that."

"I wish you wouldn't curse," Josie said. She let saliva pool in her mouth, before letting it fall to her palm. She set the cigarette there, drowning it out.

"I mean, she must, right?" He let the curtain fall closed. His face was flushed.

"That girl," Josie said, "That other girl isn't your cousin, is she?"

"Caroline?" he asked, sounding interrupted.

Josie hadn't really wanted to know her name. Caroline. Tim sat on the bed beside her. She held the blotted cigarette in her cupped hand. She touched it with one finger, rolled it over, as if trying to revive a small fish. She wondered if the lines in her hands meant anything at all, if a palm reader could tell her something she didn't already know.

Tim was looking at his own hands, the black-rimmed beds of his nails. "You still wanna," he said and nodded toward the waist of his jeans—the still open button there. He had an erection.

"You're hard?" Josie asked. There was an empty water glass at the widow's bedside; Josie scraped her palm clean against its edge. She wiped her hand dry on her jeans and motioned as if to reach for him, to open his pants. He leaned back, bracing himself, waiting. Then Josie stopped. She stood up, over him. "You're actually hard? From my mother?"

"Whatever, Post," he said, "It's all good," he straightened, running a hand through his hair. "I just came to tell you I'm near done on that truck of yours."

Josie sat back down. "Hank's truck?"

He stood and hitched up his pants, nudging the button through its slit. "Your truck now. It's not like I'm gonna charge you, if that's what that face is about," he said. He stood there for a minute, in front of her, not going—"I just need one more day on it."

He stayed there, standing above her, long enough for Josie to feel like she did want to, like she needed to.

The sky went gray late on Saturday, the air heavy and wet, and by Sunday rain was coming down in unpredictable smatterings. Rain in July.

Josie looked at Blue, wondering if this was what he had known.

She waited until Stan had gone altogether and then went down to tell Miriam that Tim had finally fixed up Hank's old truck and she needed a lift to go and pick it up. Miriam had the news on, newscasters standing around in excessive yellow rain gear.

"You believe this?" Miriam said.

The dishwasher was still open, still broken.

They drove without music, Miriam seeming lost in her own concerns, the car rattling. Tomorrow, the married guy would come over. Miriam would act amused with herself, showing him the half-dismantled dishwasher, acting like she'd been the one trying to fix it. He would pat her shoulder, kiss her. He would hire a handyman.

"I bet I can fix it," Josie said, trying to navigate the silent distance between them. Blue had his head on the console.

"Fix what?"

"The dishwasher."

"I bet you could," Miriam said in that hollow, distracted tone. Miriam stopped the car halfway across the shop's driveway. "You'll have better things to do with yourself soon enough, Josie. Finish school," her mother said. She looked tired.

Josie leaned over and kissed her on the cheek then, hoping it might mean something, but it seemed only to startle her.

Josie knew this was Tim's day off.

Only one of the truck's windshield wipers worked, luckily on the driver's side, but it was running well enough. There was a low hiss somewhere under the hood.

The needle was hovering above empty when Josie pulled into the gas station. She ran across the street to the liquor store while the truck filled up.

The guy behind the counter was wearing flip-up sunglasses, which he flicked open to ring her up. A television on the back counter was on and he was half-distracted watching the coverage of a mudslide on the Pacific Coast Highway. Then, making change, he smiled. "Where's the party tonight?" he said and touched her hand, before handing off the bottle.

Josie pushed through the door, twisting the top of the paper bag, yelling back, "I'm only nineteen, asshole."

The rain had swelled into a torrent. She ran back across the street, pulling her sweatshirt hood up over her head. She capped the gas tank and quickly fixed the passenger side mirror, which had been tilting downward as she drove, like a tired eye. Blue was in the backseat with his nose pressed to the glass. He whined and turned a circle, watching as she ran around to the other side, getting in.

She was starting the truck up when she noticed the girl, Tim's cousin, Caroline, standing at the pay phone, half soaked by rain, digging in her pockets for change. She looked up and saw Josie looking at her. A shy, tense smile passed between them.

The city lights of the valley were streaking under the sheet of rain. Josie steered the truck slowly up the canyon. Too slowly. People honked, made gestures against the glass of their windows, and then passed on the shoulder, spinning muddy rocks up from their wheels. One hit the windshield. Caroline didn't flinch.

"How'd you meet Tim?" Josie finally asked.

"How does anybody meet anybody?" Caroline said, not smiling, but showing the ridge of her teeth.

"I don't know," Josie said.

She pulled over at the lookout and parked. The rain was slowing. There was a patch of open night where the moon was waning. Josie opened the bottle, drank, then passed it to Caroline. She watched Caroline tip the passenger seat back the little it would go. She raised her feet to the dash as Josie sometimes did, though she drank more, leaving the mouth rimmed with the stamp of her lip gloss. She turned in the seat to look at Josie, asking, "Where should we go?"

"We just got here," Josie said, looking back at her, curiously.

"I've got so many places I want to go," Caroline said, her eyes shifting onto some place in the unfocused distance. The rain had stopped and the clouds were thinning, separating like white curtains drawing back for a show.

Josie smiled. "Right," she said. "Me, too."

Blue had begun to whine in the backseat. Josie left the bottle on the seat and got out and opened the door for him. She stood there in the lingering mist, watching as Blue lifted his leg again and again, marking. He sniffed about, then picked something up—a stick perhaps, a rock of clay—which he gnawed and slobbered against. What if she just let him go, let him fend for himself? Where did she want to go? There was the snap-fire of a pistol in the distance. Then another. Josie looked toward the burned-out shadow of the clapboard house. She pictured Tim there, firing into the sea of rats, their bodies black and sodden, scorched from the fire of the other night. Tim would be with Dill. Only firing cap guns, but trading stories: Tim's story being about Josie's head in his hands, moving her mouth over him while, given a breeze, he caught glimpses of her mother.

Caroline rolled down her window and handed the bottle out.

"You don't care that Tim's been seeing both of us?" Josie said then.

"Were you hoping to fight over him?" Caroline was wearing sandals and her toes, the nails painted a bright red, were flecked with mud.

"I guess not," Josie said. She hadn't asked where Caroline was going, or whom she was calling or what had happened to her car. They'd just agreed to take a drive. They were like a couple of thieves in a movie, Josie thought, like friends.

"So, let's not," Caroline said.

"Okay," Josie said.

"Okay then," Caroline said, then leaned over and turned the key in the ignition.

Blue looked up as the engine started. He'd staggered partway up the hillside. The stars were a careless white stitchwork in the now clear, dark sky. Blue would never know how to hunt and kill, but he could find his way home—he had that much animal left in him. He'd go back, Josie thought, his belly empty, and wait for someone to open the door.

Bottleneck

My father is in his car and I am in mine, but I can hear him as though he were right next to me. Technology is a wonder. He agrees and then tells me he has just walked off a plane, an on-schedule landing at O'Hare, returning from his mother's. He tells me that he retrieved his car from Kiss & Fly lot #2 (cheaper than the #1, but a train *and* a bus away) and that the first thing he did (his dead phone tethered to the car's lighter socket) is call me, "You there, 2000 miles away." He tells me these details as though the call were a gift and the details are all the thought that went into the gift. And then he says, "Hey, Kid-o!" as if we have just begun to talk, as if I am not the thirty-year-old woman that I am. Thirty, feeling like forty here.

"How is Loose Angle-ease?" he asks. "Warm?"

It is rare that he calls, rarer that I call him. Mostly holidays, remembered birthdays. I am wary when he calls like this, without my having prepared or sensed it will be him. He is chatty, upbeat. I do not trust this, but I am glad he has called when he has. I am sitting in traffic and I see up ahead what I know to be a bottleneck. I could be here for a while.

My father remarried when I was six, after my mother and I moved west: Vegas for a few months, then L.A. He bought a new house, changed jobs, and had more children: Mia, Fredrick, Susan. Mia is fourteen, the oldest. She, full of hormones, is the one to answer the phone when I do call. She speaks to me as though I were a grandmother: slow, but impatient, a little too loud.

Once I called when I knew he was at work, wanting to hear the sounds of their house with him not around: the chatter of the television, the ding of the oven timer, the boy picking on the youngest, Susan, her laughter turning to tears. But I did not ask about them or her, Mia—I know the life of a teenager—but wanted to know about him. "He seemed better last week," she'd said. "Some days he is so cranky." I wanted to know about his diet, how much he drank, if he was still smoking in the house. I wonder about these things as I am stirring the smallest pot of spaghetti, or microwaving a boxed meal for one. He frustrates her. I could hear it in her sighs and curt answers. Or it was my calling that frustrated her—the unwanted intrusion of a lesson in history.

It was always just my mom and me. A couple of boyfriends here and there—her lovers. I remember their knees, the hairy knobs of their legs, as they passed me lying on the couch with the remote extended toward the television. "Lazy fuck," one of them said. That same man slapped my mother in front of me. Thinking on it now, he may have been right about both of us.

My father and I talk about his visit to his mother, how he's trying to help her learn to use a computer, to send e-mails.

"A touchpad mouse," he says and describes how she jerks the cursor across the screen.

"Baby steps," I say, and we laugh an uneasy laugh.

What my father has done for me: Bought me a computer when it wasn't my birthday. He came here once, after I'd been in an accident. He lent me money when I had to get a place of my own. Taught me a few dirty jokes that I still recite when drunk. And when he got cancer he didn't tell me until the doctor used the word "remission."

"How do you feel, Dad?" I hear the spark of his lighter, the whistle of his inhale.

"You know. A little jet-lagged. Feel it in the bones. But that woman could drive me mad. Love her, hate her," he says, then adds, in a mumble, barely audible—am I supposed to hear? "Such are women." He laughs, so I laugh, too.

What we have in common, that I know of, are the things my mother would throw when she'd been drinking:

"A red tea kettle," he has said. "Left a lump like a plum."

I can beat that. "A VCR. Right to the stomach."

"Then that big antique brass lamp in the bedroom. Must've weighed sixty pounds."

"I don't remember it," I confess.

"You were too young."

"A softball. A vase. Pictures frames," I list.

"I didn't know."

"I was older."

"Taking stuff out on a kid," he said once.

"I was big enough," I say. "I took it fine." I let the lie of this be exposed in my tone—flat and practiced—so he might hear that I'm not just talking about her, about what gets thrown, but also about what is broken.

I have constructed his house, built it up from his small asides: "That's the kids screaming in the den . . . Fred locked Susan in the hall." I see them moving around the house clearly, but when I think about the actual logistics of what I have made, it is a circle: the kitchen becomes the den, becomes a bedroom multiplied by four, linked like a necklace with bathrooms, back to the living room which curves into the dining room. The long oak table is set with white plates, green placemats, and someone calls to Mia where she is perched on the leather lounger watching TV. His wife—I leave her faceless—puts a bib on Susan, a blue bib with lace trim. But I have not decided if they're polite, asking for the salt to be passed, or if they just reach and snatch, the little one half-naked and pawing at her liquid food.

I have no memory of my grandmother. In the three photographs I have she is as poised as a first lady, her hair white and coiffed. Her body slightly hunched, like my dad's. Like mine. Her eyes are his dark brown, her chin strong and square. Mine is the soft weak chin of my mother.

"*She* paid for that," my mother said, referring to my grandmother, looking at the delivered computer box, leaving me to set it up. I was nine, but I knew *She* meant my father was no good.

The one time he came to L.A. he stayed at the Sunburst Motel, off the 405. I've driven by it many times, seen the window of what was his room just above the deep end of the pool.

My mother dropped me off. I had my arm in a cast and sling. She said I'd never be driving her car again. The hood of it was bunched up in front of us, something scraping along the road beneath, and a windshield wiper, cracked and limp, was smacking against the glass. I thought she might park and walk me up, but she stopped traffic, reached over, and opened my door. "Room 205. Call me later."

He talked about how tall I was, "Even prettier than the pictures," and about school, "Get those grades up, Kid-o." Then he pointed to my cast and I could not help but cry. "It wasn't your fault," he said. "They had a stop sign."

I wanted to tell him that I'd been drinking, that I'd been diluting mom's bottle of Skyy, taking it in my orange juice. I wanted him to know that made it *my* fault.

I was going to the store, five blocks away. An easy walk. Beneath the stop sign, it said 4-way. But I saw him. And I saw her. She was turned around, shaking her finger at the back seat, at the kids I didn't yet know about. And he was looking in the rear view, backing her up with his eyes. I was dizzy drunk. But I knew that they weren't going to stop. I knew.

Going forty-five in a twenty-five, not even slowing for the stop sign. That's what the insurance man said.

"They do tests on the car," my dad explained. "They can tell from the way the car takes the impact how fast it was going."

I wanted to say I was glad he was here, but the words were hot and unfamiliar.

I was stopped at the sign and then I wasn't; I gunned the car, my hands at ten and two—always good about the little things when I was drunk. Still am. I felt the engine roar and the car jolt into—what I know now is—first gear, then my elbow hitting the dash, the sear of bone cracking, the skin going cold. My breasts crushed between the wheel and my weight, my neck whipped back and forth. And my heart, the pound and pump of it, swelled.

Their car, a white sedan, was up on the sidewalk, a wheel spinning against someone else's lawn. I'd driven them over and forward, buckling in the back door, the edge of the trunk. I saw the woman holding her neck. Then I saw the tops of their heads, the shiny brown tops of children's heads in the backseat. I pried at the door, yanking with my left arm, the good arm, pulling until it gave. I crawled into the back seat, gathering them up, holding them until the little girl began to scream—the sight of my arm, the bone nudging through the skin. The man stepped onto the grass. He opened the other door and pushed at me, telling me to get off. "Leave us alone," he said.

My father did not hold me when I cried. He sat rigid on the opposite motel twin bed, his hands spread open on the synthetic floral blanket. "You didn't hurt anyone," he said. "You can't feel bad. Everyone is okay."

I didn't have a swimsuit, but he wanted to go down to the pool. It was August, clear and warm. He said Chicago had been overcast and he wanted to go home with a tan. He gave me a pair of his boxer shorts and a dark gray cotton t-shirt. I changed in the bathroom. It took me a while to navigate around my cast and to figure out that by tucking the elastic band of the boxer shorts into my own underwear I could keep them up. When I came out, he was already outside. I heard him holler as he hit and emerged from the water. I'd never seen my father this close to naked before. I walked down the steps into the shallow end, keeping my arm close to my chest. I'd had the thing for a week and I was already used to directing the rest of myself around its needs. My father was smaller than I'd expected, the bones of his shoulders looking fragile beneath his skin.

"Feels good," he called out, and shook the water from his hair.

He swam down to the shallow end in a breaststroke, one foot breaking and splashing the water with each kick. I leaned against the edge of the pool.

"Listen," he said. He stood in front of me with his hands on his hips, back firm and straight, his legs spread wide, keeping most of himself submerged, his waist at water level, almost the stance of Superman. He wasn't looking at me; his eyes skimmed the edge of the pool, then the windows to the left and right. "Your mother," he started, "she thinks you should come stay with me."

"At the motel?"

"No. She thinks you should come to Chicago."

I looked at my cast then, at the place where I had signed it myself, "Christian Slater," almost illegible so that it might seem real.

"I know you don't want to. We just have the two bedrooms and Mia would wake you up ten times a night. And the weather. It's not like this—"

"Yeah, I wouldn't like that." I tried to smile.

"I'd love to have you there. You know, go to movies—"

"I know."

"Don't worry about your mom," he said. The word "your" reminding me I owned her more than anyone else, more than he would ever have to again. "I'll tell her we talked it over."

"How long were you gone?" I ask. The open spaces in our dialogue make me think there is a bad connection, an audible lag time.

"Not long enough, I tell you."

I say nothing.

"You're wondering why I'm calling," he says.

"No, no. I'm glad." I have the thought that he may be sick again, that he may have pulled the cancer back into himself.

"It's Mia."

I have no idea what Mia looks like now, fourteen, maybe sixteen. I have a Christmas card, a decade old, no other kids yet, just him and his wife and a girl with brown hair in a flouncey green dress. He is quiet. I hear the car engine turn off, not having noticed its hum until it is gone. He is crying, I hear this now, too.

"I can't go in the house."

The car behind me honks, as if there were somewhere for me to go. I have never heard my father cry before. I am embarrassed for us both. The man in my rearview is banging his hand against the side of his car, yelling profanities at the next lane over.

My father tells me that Mia does not eat, that she is going to be sent away. Locked up—this is how he puts it. "I don't want to look at her," he says. He tells me he wanted her to be gone when he came back.

She is what he cannot face. I am somehow easier. I am somewhere else, a previous life. This is why he is calling.

I think of how my mother and I screamed at one another, how I was red in the face until she picked something up, until I saw her arm arc back and I would grow calm, stand still. Maybe I even moved toward it. I think of him going to set his mother up with email. I think of all these ways we have to communicate and then there is this girl, Mia—she is my half-sister—talking with her body, saying look at what I am doing to myself, look at what we do to each other. I think of the tank tops I used to wear, showing off my bruises. I think of a man saved from cancer back to a pack a day. I think of the house I have never asked to see, that I have never been invited to visit. I think of the booze in my orange juice then and now. I think of the Sunburst Motel, just off the 405. I think of the bottleneck of traffic I wade through to go and look at a window above the deep end of a pool.

"I must have done better by you," my father says.

I am thinking of how I had screamed that day with the white sedan—the power to break a family apart, to split them in two, surging from my heart, down to my foot, to the engine, out into the lives in front of me.

The Rental

The first time Meredith Caul made love to her neighbor she rolled off him and gathered her clothes from the floor. Grasping her pants to her breasts, her thighs clenched in a feeble attempt to hide her nakedness, she scurried the fifteen feet from his front door to hers. Once inside, top and bottom locks latched, she threw herself on the couch and listened to him move around behind their shared walls, wondering if he even understood what they had done.

Meredith had recently signed a two-year lease for Unit B, 2205 Cloverfield Boulevard—just off the 10 freeway. Everyone seemed friendly enough, nodding to familiar faces, but forgoing chitchat. Unit A, however, was not a familiar face. He was the neighbor behind the curtains; that was how Meredith had begun to think of him when she got the nerve to ask Unit C about Unit A.

"He's special. Retarded, I think," Unit C said. Unit C was tall and balding, with a cleanly-groomed gray beard and a deep voice that was sometimes broken by a slight lisp—a lisp that Meredith shamed herself for stereotyping. "He has a social worker who makes sure he's got groceries and stuff."

"He doesn't go out?" Meredith asked, nervously rubbing the hem of her shirt between two fingers. This was a habit she'd had since childhood, a habit that left her not knowing what to do with the other hand. She wore button-down shirts, long-sleeved, making it easier for her to "milk"—as her friend Sarah coined it—so most people might not notice. Meredith understood not going out, often feeling her own energy was put toward keeping the world from getting in.

"His name's Peter. He won't bite." Unit C adjusted the grocery bags he'd been balancing and unlocked his door. "Go knock. Take him a pie."

"A pie?" Meredith said, considering this until the slam of Unit C's door brought her to and she plodded back to her day of filing medical claims from home for people she'd never meet.

Meredith had worked in an office for eight years as an assistant to an assistant vice president and when that assistant vice president, the third she'd served under, asked her name for the fifth time she knew there was no room for advancement. She took a course through the Learning Annex: "Eight Weeks to Filing Medical Claims from Home." Working from home seemed a natural choice. Home, the new apartment furnished with used furniture, was where she was most comfortable.

It wasn't the best neighborhood. Police sirens often sawed back and forth through the streets, but it was the safest part of the Westside she could afford. She didn't want to be in the Valley. She'd lived in the Valley before, which was reason enough to avoid it now.

There had been one incident in the laundry room when she first moved in. She did laundry late at night to ensure that she could be there alone. She didn't like parading her dirty things in front of other people and she preferred to sit in peace on the washer and feel its warmth and rattle, nearly alive. But this night there was the chatter of a helicopter, like an enormous wasp. Its spotlight waved back and forth through the window and along the wall, seeking, until it settled on her back. Meredith slid off the machine, the chemical smell of softener slipping over her, and moved to the doorway. She raised her hands up above her head and winced against the light. The helicopter paused, taking her in, then turned and fled across the night sky.

Meredith priced pick-up and drop-off laundry services, but then figured the odds were she'd never be cornered like that again. And even if she was, a little such excitement could be nice from time to time.

It was rare that Meredith went out. This was not so much a matter of the neighborhood, but because when she did leave, something pulled at her like a gauzy netting, keeping her from being fully aware of her surroundings. This was not the case with the new apartment, where she could be aware of everything, aware that everything had its place, keeping things tidy, and baking from time to time. She'd read somewhere that it was the smell of cooked food that made people feel at home. She wanted to feel at home.

Meredith could hear Unit A on the other side of her kitchen, closet, and bathroom. These were the walls that they shared. She could hear his microwave, his shower, and his stereo from the afternoon and into the evening. He kept late hours.

He isn't well, she thought. I must be more understanding.

Then, in the middle of the night, Meredith found herself sitting on the toilet sleepily listening to a song she didn't recognize when she heard the lid of the toilet behind her, Unit A's toilet, open—the clink of porcelain against porcelain. Then the plunge of water into water. She did not move, conscious now that he might be able to hear her. She waited. The pipes creaked and the faucet came on, followed by the sound of him brushing his teeth. He turned the water off, spit, tapped what she figured to be the toothbrush against the sink, and closed the cabinet. How retarded could he be? He sounded organized enough.

She couldn't sleep. She felt rattled, too aware of her lack of isolation. She worked, stopping when she heard the scrape of chair legs against wood, the TV turning on, the stereo snapping off, and then the TV dialogue turned to static. She looked at the clock. 3:01 A.M.

She filed two broken shoulders, one torn oblique, a strep throat, and a straight birth—no complications. The television's snow was still present. What if something happened to him? No one would know for days. The thought filled her with a sense of duty.

Meredith had come to know the social worker's schedule. She was a short Latina-looking woman with leathered skin, deep-set brown eyes, always sporting an alarmed look, with her hair pulled tightly back in two buns; it was a style Meredith thought a bit young for a job so loaded with responsibility, not to mention the woman's age. She was at least fifty. Her voice was squeaky, but steady, as if years of speaking to the easily distracted had left it polished to a high, even sheen. She would stay thirty minutes and always brought him a bunch of bananas. She'd been by the day before. It would be a week before he had her company again.

Meredith slipped on the red satin robe with black Chinese lettering, the one Sarah had sent from China, where she had gone to "see how other people live," over a year ago. Sarah was her last friend to move away: Sarah to China, Jill to a dude ranch, and cousin Rebecca gone quiet, no letters or calls from the Peace Corps. Meredith had given in to thinking that it was she who inspired adventure in them—not by example, but as a warning of what *not* to do, what might become of you if you stayed put. The thought often hit her like a giant wave, alarming and waking her, but leaving her more bewildered and tired out on the other side of it. She tied the robe's sash tightly and stepped out onto the balcony walkway the upper units shared.

Unit A's curtain was pulled back a body's width, as if he'd been standing there looking out at the freeway. She'd never seen his curtain open before. The refrigerator door stood slightly ajar, the light spilling onto the floor. His apartment was a mirrored image of hers. The kitchen space abnormally large, with a minimal counter but room for a dining table: his a foldable card table, hers a walnut piece with only two chairs. From the kitchen there was an unobstructed view into the living room where she saw him lying on the couch. She gathered her robe up at her throat. He didn't move. She grew calm realizing he was asleep. He was on his back, his head limp and to the side, his mouth open. He was taller than she'd imagined, filling the length of the couch, with one foot propped up on its arm, the other flat on the floor. He was lit by the television, a shivering blue light dancing across his chest, his flannel nightshirt unbuttoned. He didn't look as she'd thought he would: his features were not the eternally baby-like features she expected. No big doe-like eyes, and a rather Roman nose. His head and face were completely in proportion to his body. A very lean body, ending in long fingers and strong, wide feet, which led Meredith to believe that Unit C was ill-informed, that Unit A was not retarded at all, seemingly normal, but unable to hold a job or perhaps under house arrest. The Latina woman could be a parole officer. Meredith retreated to her apartment.

It was one week later that the social worker knocked on Meredith's door.

Meredith had lifted one of her walnut chairs to the living room window, giving her a clear view of the street down below, where the woman always parked. At 2:15 she heard the alarm clock next door. She heard his feet hit the floor and it stopped. At 2:20 the pine green Camry pulled up, hopping the curb at the building's driveway, dragging a tire along the pavement with a synthetic screech until it was a good two feet out of the red. The woman fumbled around inside the car, stacking bananas on top of papers, opening the glove box, and pulling her blazer from the backseat before nearly falling out of her opened door.

When Meredith heard the sound of heels on the stairs, she pulled her shades and pressed her ear to the wall. She waited for the three hard thuds, the way the woman always announced herself. But then came the knock at her door.

Before Meredith could say hello or ask her in, the woman was speaking.

"Sorry to disturb you. I'm Rosetta Louise." She spoke in such a hurried manner that if Meredith didn't know who she was she would have thought Ms. Louise was trying to sell her something. "I work for your neighbor, Peter." Rosetta Louise explained that she was Peter's social worker, though he was fairly self-sufficient, only slightly mentally handicapped, exhibiting some signs of autism. She went on to say that she had a conference the following week and wondered if Meredith might be willing to check in on Peter for her, as they were short-staffed. "I've noticed that you work from home," Rosetta Louise said, "and Peter would love the attention of a neighbor. This is the only day he expects company, but he counts on it."

Meredith thought about one day of company and stared at Ms. Louise's clipboard and the bananas clutched to her chest, her crisp green skirt-suit, her well-oiled legs, and spindly ankles in shiny black pumps. She looked up and saw that Ms. Louise was looking at the sleeve where Meredith was violently rubbing the fabric. It was this conversation that Meredith would mark in her memory, trying later to assign to it full responsibility for her situation.

"I'll do it," Meredith said, wishing immediately that she could pull the words back.

"He'll be thrilled. Next Wednesday. Two-ish. You know his schedule?"

Meredith nodded and Ms. Louise moved off, leaving Meredith at her open door, looking out to the humming line of traffic on the freeway, creeping along, shimmering beneath the yellowed skyline.

Meredith found herself sleeping until noon, wandering around the apartment, straightening magazines and papers, before sitting down to eat a bowl of cereal at 1:00 A.M. Every night she would lie down and hope herself tired, only to toss and listen to his music, his cooking in the kitchen, the turning on of his television, its chatter. She'd taken to trying to figure out what channel he was watching. It was a game. Curiosity was taking over.

Finally, she justified that it was his music—the same song every night. She couldn't decipher if she liked it or hated it, but she thought of it as the happy guitar and had caught herself humming along. By Saturday evening, four days earlier than necessary, remembering the suggestion of Unit C, Meredith made a banana cream pie and walked next door.

He didn't look surprised to see her at all, but said instead, "You're early," as though their scheduled meeting was not for Wednesday, but rather only fifteen or twenty minutes in the future.

"Rosetta—"

"Rosie," Peter corrected her.

"She told me you like bananas." Meredith stepped inside.

"They have potassium," he said, his voice dropping into a stiff tone, as if speaking in a commercial for bananas. His hair was a rusty blond.

"Do you like pie?"

"Everybody likes pie." Peter sat down on his couch and it seemed to Meredith he was waiting for her to do something. She told him that she had made a banana cream pie and asked if he'd like to try it. He said yes. She found herself nervously opening drawers and cabinets, looking for forks and plates. Thoughtlessly, she opened the refrigerator. She was bent down into the cool cleansing air, debating if she could muster the calm she needed to sit down and eat with this man, and he was a man—odd, yes, but more handsome than she wanted to fully consider—when she heard from over her shoulder, "That looks really good."

"Peter," she said, remaining very still. She had read that in the event of an attack a woman should give her assailant her name, that personalization could dissuade him.

"Yes," Peter said.

"My name is Meredith."

"I know that," he said.

Nearly finished with the pie, after watching the end of a movie-of-the-week and a talk show rerun, Meredith remembered the song. He told her it was Django Reinhardt and his mouth lifted in a grin that moved up into his eyes. One of his front teeth was larger than the other, the only asymmetry about his face, a suddenly endearing inconsistency. Meredith had shied away from meeting his eyes all night—jumping up to get them second and third pieces of pie and glasses of water at commercial breaks—but now she couldn't help but smile back. She asked him to play the song for her and he brought out a small tape deck and set it on his lap. They listened. Meredith's foot tapped beneath her empty plate, the fork rattling along. Peter kept his eyes closed, his head bobbing back and forth—more against the beat than with it, but happily, joyfully. When it ended, Meredith thought it was over too quickly. Peter did not open his eyes. She looked at him. He had pushed his lips together, into a kiss. Meredith leaned over and let her lips graze his. Like a mother to a son, she thought, and pictured Rosie doing this in some unaffected, foreign way. But Meredith felt an unfamiliar heat beneath her skin.

"Merri-deth," he said, "Merri-deth."

She laughed at the way he said her name, making it sound awfully big and important. She kissed him again.

The first time they made love Meredith panicked. It was the following day, Sunday, the day after they'd kissed. She'd woken up and dressed immediately. It was against her normal routine of coffee and the paper, but she wanted to get to the store. She needed bananas. She'd told Peter she would teach him how to make banana bread.

He seemed disinterested in the measuring of ingredients, but enjoyed dipping his finger against the spoon to taste the batter. They watched television together while the bread baked, the smell filling in around them. Meredith laughed at the jokes, but Peter seemed to laugh between them. It took her carefully studying him and what was on the screen to realize that he laughed when there was a picture hung crookedly or a person dropped a pencil or when a glass on a table had gone from full to empty without cause, things Meredith found almost imperceptible. She wondered if Sarah felt similarly about meeting people in a foreign country.

When the bread was ready, Meredith asked him to lift the card table with her, to move it in front of the couch, so they could sit and eat; he had only one chair. The change seemed to excite him. He sat up tall and straight and placed his hands flat on the table.

"This is great," he said. "People being together."

Meredith set the table, already knowing her way around his kitchen, and placed the bread on a cutting board with a soft stick of butter.

"Do you have friends?" she asked, cutting and laying a wedge in front of him.

"Rosie," he said. "And you? Merri-deth?" he asked, cautiously, his scraggly eyebrows lifting.

"I'm your friend. Yes," she said. "I want to be your friend." She reached over and wiped a fleck of bread from his cheek.

She saw him reach for the bread knife, but she was looking at her own hands, at the dark purple birth mark on her wrist, showing at the edge of her shirt sleeve, when he cut the bread again and sliced into his thumb. He did not cry out, but held it up, as if to admire it, the blood running to his arm. Meredith, made slightly more panicked by his calm, pushed at him and held the hand up over his head as she ushered him to the bathroom.

"Will I die?" he asked, as she sat him on the toilet.

"Of course not." She paused and met his eyes to reassure him.

"If I do," he said, in a voice lifted from a TV drama, "you must go on."

Meredith tried, but could not help but laugh. Peter did too.

On the bottom shelf she found a first aid kit. On her knees in front of him she pulled his hand under the faucet, washed it, and dabbed antiseptic. It was a deep cut.

She told him to hold it up, above his heart, to slow the bleeding.

"Does it hurt?"

"Not above my heart."

It was his other hand that reached down and touched her hair. She'd been in this position before, but not in a very long time and never had she found her head so close to a man's center without the touching of her head seeming overly insistent. She nuzzled the inside of his thigh with her nose and mouth, until she found herself unbuttoning his pants. She did not look at him until she had led him back to the couch. He slouched down, as though all strength had left him, and Meredith—she would try to know how for a long time—found herself in his lap, her own hands taking his and moving them up and under her shirt.

Meredith knew she wasn't pretty. She was short and wide around the middle, her face too round and her hair—not straight or curly—a tangle of thin wire. A man had not touched her in years. She'd been kissed in a bar a year ago and that man had begun to grope her breast before Sarah finally called her away. But that feeling had been different. Peter didn't weaken her.

She lay on her couch, her clothes off and bunched around her, listening to Peter move around behind their shared walls, wondering if he understood what they had done. She told herself it wouldn't happen again. That she would go over there on the Wednesday she was due, three days away, and act as if nothing had happened. If he told Rosie, whom would Rosie believe anyway?

At first he was insatiable and Meredith found him too noisy. He was always asking questions and clumsily laying his hands on places that had no allure, no excitement for her: the handle of flesh at her side, the back of her thigh—squeezing it until she had to say something—and her ears. He had a thing about her ears, not kissing them, but touching them, fingering every fold. He could be painfully annoying, but she loved the smell of his skin—that heady man smell. And she soon learned that she could tell him what to do and what not to do without upsetting him, as long as she used the same tone of voice. After she'd moved above him, atop his plaid comforter, watching his face for the moment his smile turned to something deeper, almost laughter, she would roll off him and he would brush her hair and rub her hands and feet, unphased by such a request, allowing her to be the one to give over to laziness.

She'd been very careful with the neighbors, checking and double-checking the walkway and driveway before entering or exiting Unit A. She'd kept them both on his up-at-noon-asleep-before-sunrise schedule and made sure the blinds were drawn all day as they had been before.

But it was Tuesday night when Unit C looked at Meredith sideways and she felt sure she'd been found out. Unit C had looked as if he wanted to say something; his mouth opened, drawing in a breath, but then he only exhaled with a shake of his head. Meredith wanted to feel him out, but she couldn't figure a viable reason to knock on his door. She went to Peter. He looked at her hands, saw they were empty, and sat back down on the couch.

"I'm hungry," he said.

"I can't make anything now, Peter." Meredith stroked the edge of her sleeve between two fingers.

"I'm hungry, Merri-deth."

She realized he'd stopped cooking for himself altogether. "I think Unit C knows."

Peter turned the channel.

"Did you hear me?" she asked. "What do we do?"

The gravity of the situation hit her: Ms. Louise, Rosie, would be there in 24 hours. She needed to know that Peter would not let on, that he could keep from saying something inappropriate, but she didn't want to distress him. She sat down beside him and watched him watching television. He unfastened his pants and looked at Meredith.

"Not now," she told him.

Everything, all at once, she noticed everything, everything that was out of place because of her, how she'd moved in on Peter's—she remembered Rosie's voice now—"his routine." The sheets. Why hadn't she washed the sheets? All the extra toilet paper that had been used. Would Rosie notice something like *that*? What about the trash? The trash was full of broken eggshells, onion skins, apple cores, and the trays from frozen dinners—that was at least in keeping with his "routine." But the Chinese take-out cartons, her plastic cups from her low-fat yogurts, and an excessive number of browned banana peels. The condoms. Could she get the trash down to the alley? She'd have to go by Unit C. He'd be at the window, surely.

Peter was pawing at her breast, mindlessly, his eyes on the evening news.

"Touch me, Merri-deth," Peter said. Meredith didn't move. There was a high-speed chase on the television, as usual. A pale blue car this time, its sides dented as if it had squeezed through a narrow space. A camera on a helicopter followed it as it flew through one intersection and then another, each time the oncoming traffic narrowly missing it, swerving left and right, sometimes blindly knocking into one another, but always avoiding the one car that needed to be stopped. Meredith turned the volume down. She could hear sirens. The chase was nearby.

"Please, Merri-deth," Peter said, running his fingers through her hair.

"Quickly," she said, surrendering, letting him pick her up, his left arm slipping beneath her knees, the other cupping her shoulders.

He laid her down on the rumpled sheets. She slipped her shoes off and grabbed his arm, leading him to the hem of her skirt. He started to run his fingers along the inside of her thighs, the way she'd shown him, but she pulled him down onto her, grabbing at his jeans, tugging them away from him. Her body was tight, tense, her back and thighs clenched. He touched her hair and stroked her cheek, his eyelids fluttering, his skin red with blood and heat. Meredith pushed with her thigh and pushed with her hand against him and rolled him over onto his back, hanging on with all her strength, she stayed with him. She took his wrists in her hands and held him, keeping him like that.

There had been no alarm set for 2:15—one more routine abandoned—but Rosie's knock came with its same persistent three thuds. And then again. And a pause. Then the metal to metal of a key meeting its lock, as loud as if it were just beside Meredith's ear. They had fallen asleep.

"This, this?" Rosie said. She kept saying it, over and over, looking at them, until she shoved Meredith away, simultaneously pulling Peter up, covering his bare body with herself, standing between them, in her taut green suit.

The car chase on the news was a stolen vehicle. A police officer happening to pull up the plate only after witnessing it rolling through a stop sign—the California roll. Commonplace crime. If Meredith had had Peter in that pale-blue car, she would have maneuvered it more deftly, with real purpose.

Peter rested his head on Rosie's shoulder and started humming.

"This is abuse," Rosie finally managed.

"It is," Meredith said, thinking that there was never enough gas, that the chase always ended.

Detour

Josie brought a girl with her. Caroline. A rusty-haired girl with quick eyes and fidgety hands.

Hank found the girl, Caroline, in the kitchen at daybreak, fixing coffee and remarking on the silence and how she wasn't used to there not being any sirens or car horns. He thought her too young for coffee, but he was glad to see it ready. She followed him through the barn while he pieced out hay flakes and mixed bran. She said she liked the way the horses smelled. "Their shit and everything." She liked to talk, but not too much, and she had good instincts, walking a wide berth when he moved a stallion to the turnout.

The morning's work done, Hank settled on the back deck with a fresh cup. Caroline took up the chair beside him, breathing overly deep breaths, suggesting her enjoyment of the place. A field of flaxen grasses stretched from the deck clear to the mountain ridge in the far distance, unbroken except for two scrub oaks, their shadows lying long. Bessa, the old hound mix, had staked out her morning shade there. Earlier, she'd given a low growl when he passed by with Caroline. He was hoping Bessa would perk up when she saw Josie again. If her nose was sound enough to know Josie still.

The little white dog hopped up on the deck with a dead sparrow in its mouth. Caroline gave a short, shocked inhale.

Hank patted the little dog's head and the dog dropped the bird and backed up, tail wagging, as if he were going to throw it out into the field for him to retrieve again. One wing was broken and the neck snapped, but the flesh had not been punctured and Hank figured the credit was owed to a hawk.

The girl asked to see the bird. Hank set it in her cupped hands. She fingered its feathers and held it in a way that amused him, as if she were going to learn something from looking at it. He told her about how that little white dog had shown up one day, that there was a river nearer to the main road and sometimes people took puppies there for drowning. He figured this one had held on and found his way here.

"You should name him," Caroline said. "Something princely. Or heroic."

He didn't tell her he hadn't named him because he felt doing so was going to bring him that much closer to having to put Bessa down. Josie was still asleep.

"Should I wake her?" Hank motioned up to the second bedroom where he'd carted their single duffel bag the night before.

He hadn't yet figured if Caroline was Josie's lover. It had been five, six years since he and Josie's mother split. Josie was near fifteen then. That was the last time he'd seen Josie, let alone talked to her. He'd written since the move, but she never answered his letters. Still, she knew where to find him when she needed to, hadn't she?

"Josie needs eight hours or she's just bad company," Caroline said. She had the little dog on her lap, prone and subdued under the stroke of her hand. Bessa was a silhouette under the oak, snapping at the flies drawn to her ears. It was still temperate, but the flies suggested heat was nearing.

"You know Josie pretty well then?"

"We've been on the road about three weeks, but you really get to know somebody on the road, don't you?"

Caroline was a slight girl, not terribly pretty, her red-brown hair seemed misplaced against her olive complexion. But there was something calming about her, a warmth about her company. Hank could see how she and Josie would end up together.

Josie was always a little on edge, jumpy and muscled even as a little kid. She was looking more and more like her mother when he'd left: long dark hair and almond shaped blue eyes, striking, but also somewhat masculine. She always had a kind of power about her. It wasn't confidence so much—he thought her insecure, really—but something further down the spectrum, something more unpredictable, more animal. It gave her some advantage with the horses, an authority that Hank envied.

"Does Josie still ride?" he asked.

Caroline shook her head, eyes down. "Not since you left."

Hank took a sip of his coffee. It was cool. "She's still angry with me then."

"We're here," Caroline said, not looking at him, as though she'd already anticipated and resolved herself to this line of conversation. They'd talked about him, clearly. Hank had an ambiguous feeling. Uncertainty? Helplessness. Unsure. He felt unsure. Unsure that Josie was even in his house at all. That she were truly upstairs, sleeping. There was something tenuous, even phantom-like about her arrival the night before, like he'd dreamt it. But here was this friend of Josie's, Caroline. Proof.

"Did I hear her working on that truck last night? You're brave girls driving that thing from L.A." The night before, he'd heard the knock and sputter of the truck—his old truck—before they'd made the turnin and then, by the porch light, seen the clot of smoke that hung around them.

"She thinks she'll have it fixed today."

"You don't sound too confident."

Caroline shrugged. "Either way. I like it here. It's good to be somewhere else."

"Where you headed?" he asked.

"All over," she smiled.

An animal rustled in the brush and the little dog flipped over, snapping to attention, and took off into the field. Caroline jumped up with him and followed him to the end of the porch, yelling, "Go get 'em, Richard." She turned back to Hank, pivoting on her bare feet.

"Oh, no," she said. "Not that. Not right at all."

"You'll figure it," Hank said. "I'm sure."

Josie didn't come down until after Hank had put the mares out to pasture and they'd started fixing sandwiches for lunch.

"I need a part," Josie said.

The night before, Hank had failed to see that Josie had cut her hair boy-short and died it black. There was a thin silver ring in the side of her nose. Her left arm was sunburned, perhaps from leaning on the window, driving. And the pale right arm, the bicep, was crisscrossed with a thick black tattoo, the flesh around it pink and shiny, as if she'd recently pulled away the bandaging. All morning he'd been picturing Josie five years ago, with her hair a rope of a braid down her back, her cheeks and the bridge of her nose swept with freckles. This shock of her now, actually seeing her, must have been evident on his face. She looked smug, pleased.

"It's pretty," he said, pointing to the tattoo.

"It took two sittings. It's tribal. You're supposed to hate it."

She'd left a message on his machine an hour before they drove in. She'd started to leave a number for him to call back if he didn't want her to come by, but the machine had cut her off—he was glad not to have the choice.

He thought to say she was wrong, that he did like the tattoo, that it suited her—though it didn't—and that she looked good, healthy, even though she looked like she'd been taking care of everyone but herself. He understood, however, that she would prefer he acted as she was, as though his new place, his home was just a detour.

"Can I take your car to town?" she asked.

"Hell, you can take a horse if you want." He wasn't always such a jackass.

"Care, are you coming with me?"

"Can I eat first?"

"Fuck it," Josie said. "I'll be back." She grabbed Hank's keys from the counter and strode out.

Caroline offered Hank the bag of chips. This was the chaos of women. It had been years since he'd known it. He said nothing to Caroline, taking his sandwich and heading back to the barn.

Miguel was forking out the mare's stalls, always trying to work when they were empty, having been kicked too many times.

"You got company," Miguel said, pointing in the direction of the house. "Pretty ladies."

"It's my ex's kid and her lesbian lover, *comprende*?" Hank struggled with his boots, trying to stomp them on, until Miguel handed him the boot hooks, smiling. "Quit standing around. Go give the foals another flake or polish the tack. Do something."

Hank ate, then groomed and saddled the new stallion himself. He had him round on the bit and his back flat and solid when he noticed Caroline there, leaning on the rail. He patted the horse on the neck, whispered to him that he'd have Miguel wet-wrap him, and walked over to Caroline.

"Beautiful," Caroline said. The little dog had followed her out. It was the closest Hank had seen the dog get to a horse without barking.

"I'm sorry about earlier, for taking off at lunch," Hank said.

"I understand," Caroline said, reaching out to touch the stallion's neck. "Josie's back. Pissed, too. They said they'd have to order the belt. Could take a week."

"Can I ask something, so we're clear?"

"Anything," she said.

"Are you and Josie together? I mean, *together*?"

"That's too bad," Caroline said. The little dog started barking then ran off. "Josie said you'd probably think that. That you didn't know her well enough not to think that." The stallion stomped at the ground. "She was apologizing for you."

"Fuck," Hank said. Miguel was standing at the end of the barn, leaning on his rake. "Miguel, get to work. Why am I paying you?"

"Lesbians," Miguel said, taking a handtowel to his face as if perspiring at the thought, before letting out a whistle.

"Shit, I'm sorry," Hank said, but Caroline was smiling.

Caroline waited while Hank put the stallion up. The little dog met them again in the field as they walked back. They walked in silence. Josie was in the distance, on the deck.

She was bent over Bessa, stroking the dog's long ears flat. They stepped onto the deck.

"You need to put her down," Josie said, not looking up. "She's miserable. She looks like shit."

"She's all there," Hank said. Bessa lifted her head at the sound of his voice and waddled over, her hind joints stiff, her paws dragging. Caroline went to pet her, but Bessa growled and leaned into Hank's legs. "She's fine, Josie. She isn't hurting."

Bessa had been Josie's dog. She'd brought her home as a pup, having found her wandering the stables where they used to board the horses. Hank knew she didn't want him to, but Miriam, Josie's mother, had asked him to take the dog with him when he left. He was always the one taking care of Bessa anyway, so he did. Part of him had thought it would make Josie talk to him again, that she would need to find out how the dog was doing and they'd get back on track, but she never did. And now here she was, telling him he should have put the dog out of her misery by now. That he was being selfish.

The next day the little white dog scrounged up a field mouse and brought it into the kitchen. Josie spent most of the day in the driveway, working on the truck, though they all knew there wasn't much to do without the belt.

The day after that Hank caught sight of the hawk he thought had been doing the little dog's killing. He and Caroline fed the horses together in the morning and she helped him put the mares out. They were back on the porch, watching the sky, when the hawk dove into the field, swam up with something thrashing in its mouth, and then dropped it. It spun end over end through the clean blue canvas of the midmorning sky.

"Why would it do that?" Caroline asked.

"Could be he's training. He looks small. Could be the mother hawk is watching somewhere and they aren't hungry. Just practice kills."

"You know a lot about hawks."

He knew nothing. He was making it up, having a little fun. He smiled at her and she smiled back. The little dog ran off into the field, sniffing out the hawk's disposables.

"You should ask Josie to ride with you," Caroline said then.

"You said she doesn't ride anymore."

"She also doesn't have to fix that truck herself. We've got enough money for a mechanic."

"Self-reliance is a bottomless resource," he said. He felt Caroline smirking beside him. "What?"

"Sometimes Josie sounds like a fortune cookie too."

Hank couldn't bring himself to form the question, but he brought Josie a sandwich and told her there were three horses that still needed exercising that day. He told her that one was a gelding, if she'd feel more comfortable with a gelding.

"I can ride a stallion. I can ride your ornery mares, too. Give me what you don't want to handle," she said.

"I always liked your sass, Josie."

He loaned Josie a pair of chaps that he'd worn in his leaner days and had Miguel saddle up the smaller stallion and the gelding. He started to hand the reins of the gelding to Josie, but she took the stallion from him. He'd thought she might. This stallion was a 16-hand chestnut and Hank had ridden him the night before and figured he'd be a little quieter for it. "Tonka's Play Thing," he told her, introducing the horse by its papered name.

They walked around the ring on a loose rein, but Tonka didn't take to the proximity of the gelding and Hank steered him off.

"Care said you just got him from Germany," Josie said. "You'd think they'd have beat that behavior out of him by now."

"Swiss trainer," Hank said. "He responds to tongue-clucking better than a spur."

Josie laughed and Hank realized how pleased he was, even comfortable, being out there with her again. He watched her tighten up the reins and settle into her seat. It was a natural posture for her and she slipped the stallion into a trot with ease.

"He's a good fit for you," he said to her.

But after she circled the ring a few laps, Hank saw her heels lifting. She was clenching in the knees more than the thigh, her strength not distributed in the way it once was when she'd been riding daily. When Hank left Miriam, selling off the two old geldings, taking only the mare with him, Miriam said it was for the best. *I wanted a father for Josie, but I never wanted to be a wife.*

"Your ring slopes down over here," Josie called out.

"I know. I always have to pick their heads up through there."

"I could help fill it in," Josie said.

"I could use some good help." Hank sat in the center and watched her pick up a canter. She leaned forward too far, egging him on like she was heading for a fence. "Sit back," Hank called, a little hesitant to correct her.

Tonka threw his head up then. Josie smacked back into the saddle and, feeling the sudden weight of her seat, Tonka kicked out his back legs and threw her to the dirt. Josie reached with her right arm, bracing the full brunt of her fall on one wrist, snapping it back, her elbow buckling into her chest. She did not holler in pain or surprise, only let the air escape from her, audibly, with the impact. Tonka ran for the barn.

Miguel had managed a month of working under the local veterinarian, years ago, and he'd learned to set a leg, so when Josie refused a doctor, Hank insisted she let Miguel splint the wrist, just in case there was a fracture. Caroline had been throwing sticks for the little dog out in the field and she had run over, having heard Hank yell out that Josie should lie still. Now she was sobbing over Josie.

"I'll be fine," Josie told her.

Hank could see Josie being something of a mother to Caroline, or an older sister.

"It's not so bad," Miguel said. "No blood. Always good." Miguel turned tail at the sight of blood—not a lick of help during foaling season.

"I can feel it swelling," Josie said.

"Oh, Jesus," Caroline moaned.

Josie actually seemed a little glad to be hurt, as if she'd come through some initiation, as though the fall had loosed some tension from her, sent it drifting out of the barn, away from them. A quiet passed between the four of them, with Caroline holding Josie's good hand, Miguel taping up the splint, and Hank bent at Josie's feet, watching her eyes, waiting for her gaze to settle on him.

"You remember that Palomino that threw me against the rail. Everybody thought my back was broken," Josie said. "Part quarter horse. What a nag that thing was."

"I don't know what possessed me to get a horse for your mother." There, he thought, an opening—let's discuss Miriam, let's discuss all I did for her and how little there was in return.

"He never even told her about the horse," Josie said to Caroline, as if he weren't there. She got up and started undoing the chaps with her good hand, rushing through it, fumbling with the cinching. "That was easier than knowing she didn't want it." She motioned to Caroline to get up, never meeting Hank's eyes, and they left him there with Miguel, who was stupidily grinning.

There was a note when he went back to the house. They'd taken his car into town to have dinner. It was not Josie's handwriting. The house felt still. It was a nervous stillness, as though something hid in the shadows. He'd gotten used to not being alone too easily.

He had to lift Bessa's back end with a towel to help her into the house and over to her bowl where she laid back down. He poured chicken broth over the kibble to make it easier for her to chew and used his hands to feed her. Looking into the grayed expression of her drooping eyes he couldn't tell if she recognized him or not. She's fine, Josie. Just fine.

He fixed himself a bourbon, thinking he would wait up for them, that they would all sit out back and have a drink, turn the page as it were. A single drink gave him this feeling of possibility. "We're here," Caroline had said when he asked if Josie was still angry. He poured himself a second. He picked up the flashlight and swished the light across the lawn, watching the little dog chase after it—confused when he couldn't grab it in his jaws.

Hank heard the front door open and he held the light still, the dog pouncing up and down on the globe of bright grass. Surely they saw him sitting out there, but he couldn't bring himself to call after them, and they didn't stop. There was the creak of the wooden stairs beneath their feet and the slow, careful click of their door being closed, as if to go undetected. He poured himself another.

"Hank? Hank, it's Caroline." She was standing at the foot of his bed.

"What is it?" He sat up, still feeling that his clothes were wet. It was rare that he dreamed, but when he did it was always underwater. He was still at the bottom of the pond when Caroline woke him. He'd not yet felt the tightening of his lungs.

"I can't sleep," she said, sitting down by his knees. "I have to tell you something or I won't ever sleep."

"Is Josie all right?"

"I think so. But this is my fault." She put her hand on his leg, without hesitation. "I told Josie that you didn't think she could ride anymore. Do you see what I did? I challenged her."

"I get it," Hank said, sitting up, feeling for the lamp, but Caroline reached over and stopped him.

"I just want you two to make up, for Josie to see we can all be okay."

"One big happy family," Hank said. Through the blue darkness he could make out her silhouette. The slope of her shoulders, the wetness of her eyes.

"Yes."

"But we're not family, Caroline."

"I know," she said. "But I still can't sleep."

His eyes grew accustomed to the room, to her there. She was in a pale pink shirt and only her underwear. She stared back, a question in her eyes. The phrase *communal loneliness* came to Hank, though he couldn't place it, could only see it in the gentle way the girl's lips were parted, as though she had everything to say, but not the language to begin. Her hand was still on his leg and he let her move toward him, touching his hip. He let her bend over him. He let himself feel the frame of her in his arms, her hair across his shoulders, but he stopped her when she went to kiss him, bringing his fingers to her lips, only allowing himself to hold her, to have that comfort, briefly.

Caroline was on the back porch in the morning, curled in a chair, her knees drawn up in the wool blanket from the couch. There was no suggestion of Josie about. Something about the way Caroline was, a stillness as if a part of the landscape, told Hank she'd been there the rest of the night, since he had asked her to go.

"I'm having the truck towed into town," he said. "Josie can't fix it with that wrist."

"True," Caroline said, not turning around.

The little dog, he saw now, was curled beside her in the chair.

"You girls take him with you," Hank said. He touched the animal's head.

"The hawk is back," she said and pointed into the clouds. "Louie brought me a field mouse already. He's a smart dog."

"He likes you," Hank said. "Louie's a decent name."

"Do you even know why Josie is angry with you?"

He looked out to the empty pasture. He wanted to set the mares out, to have his usual morning, to be there, moving amongst them, feeling the warmth of their necks, the heat of their breath. He wanted to say that Josie was here, so she couldn't be that angry.

"I'm not her real father," he said. "It confuses things."

A commotion of dishes, a cupboard slamming shut: Josie was in the kitchen.

Caroline pushed the little dog off her. "It confuses you," she said and went inside.

Hank was feeding in the barn when the tow arrived. The truck was fixed, one town over, in a matter of hours. He was still in the barn, helping Miguel wash down the mares, when they returned. He was starting back across the field, toward the house, when the single black duffel dropped to the ground, pitched out from the window. Caroline, already below, hoisted it up and into the bed of the truck. Hank felt the weight of his body as though he'd just woken, as if his clothes were heavy with water, everything slowed down. The screen door swung closed behind Josie and there were the two distended honks of the truck's horn, the same way they'd arrived, an almost hopeful sound. The little dog started running after the truck. The truck stopped and Caroline got out. She turned and waved to Hank—a big mocking parade sort of wave, smiling. Louie jumped into the front seat, a happy barking dog. The truck sputtered, but then kicked into gear, and they were gone, just like that, back on the main road.

Earlier in the day, Hank had asked Miguel to dig him a hole under the oak tree, but now Hank thought better of it, knowing he would have to look at that tree every morning, and so he carried Bessa into the field.

He wondered how long it would take Caroline to tell Josie about last night or if she already had, while they were stuffing their things back together in their bag. He'd never gotten a handle on the dynamics of female relationships, but he could feel that this girl liked having some sway over Josie, that she was a little threatened by Josie's strength and needed to find some control; the way scared people rode thoroughbreds, always shortening the reins. He'd allowed Caroline that control when he held her in his bed and he figured she and Josie wouldn't be much farther along when Caroline would spin it into more than it had been, confirming for Josie that he was as weak as she thought he was, that he took the easy way out of things. The way it had been easier to leave and just start over, new horses and all. The way it had been easy to hold a girl he barely knew instead of Josie, instead of hugging her and telling her she would always be his daughter.

He touched Bessa's ears, rubbing the fur flat, and kissed her head. He set the rifle down and curled himself beside her, feeling the labored rise and fall of her chest against his own. He wasn't going to shoot his dog. He wasn't going to watch her be picked over by birds or bury her or drown her in the river. So he was selfish.

The day he told Josie that he wasn't just moving out, but away, she said, "Everybody needs somebody. Just one other person who is as faithful to them as they are to themselves." It was a cryptic or maybe mature statement, but he'd gone and taken it for what he needed it to be: her blessing for him to leave Miriam, for him to go. He hadn't let himself understand how she'd been saying everything to the contrary. He closed his eyes against the sun. When he opened them, there were two hawks overhead, coasting circles around one another.

Sleight of Hand

It was summer. I was newly twelve, though my father—just before going—had said, "You are almost a woman." And then there was a man, the man who kept me for several days. A friend of my father's—that is what he told me. He was in the house before I was, waiting. He knew my name.

"Dolores," he said, as though he'd just finished setting the table.

"Who are you?" I asked, putting my hand to my throat to feel the question.

"Charlie," he said.

He knew that I lived alone with my father, that my mother was dead to us, and that my father would be away for some days. He had a southern accent, a long draw on the o's of my name. My father had taken me to Mississippi when I was ten or so, to see the casinos that line the muggy, mosquitoed coast; not to show me where, but how he grew up, the rattle and click of the roulette wheel. I remembered lunch with a man who was not a relative, a man who had a southern accent, but I could not find his face, only that he sat on his hands while he chewed.

"Charlie," he said again. "Your dad's friend."

I've read that a gambling addict is someone who remembers the triple cherries, the quadruple sevens, the double-down that had him ahead five-times what he walked in with, but who is quick to forget all the other plays, the losses that are inevitably more frequent than the gains.

My father was a gambler, a card-counter, but also a magician. "There is no magic," he would say, "only the sleight of hand—something taken away is replaced by something else."

My friend Loraine is staying with me now. Loraine is a real estate agent four hours north of here, but she wanted to be out of town while her soon-to-be ex-husband moved his things, taking them to Self Storage, before parking his car in the same driveway Loraine waited in a month ago—needing to confront him right outside the other woman's apartment.

Self Storage. This is a phrase that always stops me.

Last week, over dinner, Loraine said she was mad at me, upset that I was selling the house and that I hadn't asked for her help.

In the car it was, "A woman with a house is more marketable, Dolores."

"She has curb appeal?" I asked, already tired of the conversation.

I told her she could field the offers. I would fire the agent I'd just hired.

"It's a mistake," she said. "What about the dog? You need the yard."

"The dog," I explained, "doesn't stay in the yard."

The dog has taken to jumping the fence whenever I leave, roaming the streets, mapping out all the alleyways, until he hears the familiar squeal of my brakes and comes bounding from one direction or the other, tongue limp with thirst, his paws up on the window.

I wondered then if he would recognize Loraine's car, if he watched me get into it earlier that night. I scanned the road ahead, worried her car would be the car to hit him. We turned the corner and found he was waiting at the door.

"But where will you go?" she asks, teary, as if this house is the only house.

The house I once shared with my father—and then my father's friend, for those five days—is small and open, each room easily visible from every other. But Charlie kept me tied down in one place, on my own bed, my mouth full with his undershirt. The daylight reflected off the water of the canals, skipping crescent winks across the all-white walls, letting me know when a rowboat had passed, that there was the ripple of another life just outside. A flock of wild parrots—lost from their cages—watched and jittered at the window, squawking asides. At night there was nothing: grayness, the weight of a full grown man stranded across me, sleeping, wrestling terrors, then sinking deeper, stinking of our vinegar: booze, smoke, sweat, and the metallic stench of blood.

I had loved this house, with its all-white walls, months-grown grass, the musky smell of algaed rocks at the canal's edge. It had been the new house, the new deal; the old brick one having gone to a man with a bowler hat and a pair of aces.

Loraine insists I look at condos. I find the experience of walking through other people's homes disconcerting. Or maybe it is the arousal I feel that is disconcerting. After pacing our way through several, we slow and linger in the last one. The bedrooms are on the second floor, the living room, kitchen, and dining room downstairs, living and sleeping kept neatly separated. There is a view of the building's courtyard: four thin trees struggling, leaning south, searching the last bits of daylight, two wrought iron chairs, flaking paint, no table, and a concrete birdbath gone green in the center.

"It's still too much space," I say, having complained about the size of the house I now have to myself. There is an unending surprise, not finding anyone else curled in a corner of the rooms I do not set foot in for weeks at a time.

Not long ago, the flowers outside the bedroom window—birds of paradise—attracted a sickness: small moldy freckles running up their orange heads and down their dense, gray-green spines. A part of me was glad, happy to watch them brown and wilt with disease; I have often found them too haughty, too strikingly beautiful with their manly pride.

I sit down at the baby grand piano in the condo's living room, picturing how it will be lifted out over the balcony, exhaling a song as it is lowered to the ground.

Loraine is leaning on the mantel of the faux fireplace. "I don't know if I can go back to my house," she is saying, touching the picture frame around someone else's family. "There will be too many things missing."

"It's only magic," I sing, and improvise the tune.

Loraine will go back, this house will sell, and soon enough the dog will wander farther than his memory is long.

I will go and look for my father's friend. I will move toward him with the whirl and click of roulette. I will rest my hand on the felt beside his facedown cards. I will ask him what he has won that day and he will mouth, "Dolores," knowing me at once. I will tell him to take me in, to let me live with him, and cook for him. To let me keep that part of myself—that part he took and replaced with something else—company.

Inheritance

Drew's parents died as they had lived, one after the other, in a rather organized and unagonizing way. First his father, in early October, a stroke over his *Post* and tea. His mother followed six weeks later, before the holidays, in her sleep. It fit them, painless and quiet.

"So considerate," a woman in eggplant black said at his mother's wake, caressing the back of Drew's hand as one might a smooth stone.

They'd had Drew late in life, as something of an afterthought, and he felt they'd raised him in this way as well, in between lunches and bridge. Like Drew, they were only children, leaving him without aunts or uncles, no cousins; no one. But they'd woven together a vast group of friends in their long marriage and so they'd found it odd when Drew needed therapy in college and that loneliness could be a part of the diagnosis, let alone something that warranted a prescription. They took to looking at him as if he were on the other side of a dirty window. "Incorrigible," his father muttered, seeing Drew with his pills in hand. His father, Dr. Washburn, had retired from medicine over a decade earlier and Drew understood *incorrigible* was more of a reference to the state of medicine than to Drew—yet somehow this, the absence of a personal insult, was more hurtful.

Then Drew decided he wanted to be a photographer and not a physician, like his father.

"Say again," his father insisted, over waffles.

Drew thought, at the time, that he meant a photojournalist, that he would travel the world—revealing the miseries of mankind—in cargo pants, with a battered camera bag slung over his shoulder.

"All right then," his mother said.

"How romantic," his father said.

His mother wrote him a check for two thousand dollars to purchase equipment. His father felt this was not the sort of career for which you took courses; you were either good or you weren't. He bought a Mamiya 645, a 55 and an 80 mm lens, a brick of Kodachrome 200. He photographed abandoned barns, cemeteries. And then portraits of the men who worked at the 76 station, Avedon-like portraits, but saturated with color. "These aren't bad," his father said, fanning through the proofs. "More," he said. But then his father died, and then his mother, and this left Drew well-off with a house, and the house suggested to him, in its quiet old yellow house kind of way, that he might not exist outside of it. And so, at twenty-three, he was alive, yet haunting his parents' home. This was how he described the feeling to Caroline and she seemed to understand.

She was the first response to the rental ad he'd been running since February. It was early April. She phoned around noon and said she would be by in a few minutes. The last of winter's ice was dripping from the eaves. He grilled a sandwich, leaning into it with the spatula, and waited.

As he fingered the last of the greasy crumbs, a spear of ice thawed and slipped from the rain gutter. He heard it—the clack-clack-clack, as it slid down the pipes' ribbing—just in time to look up and watch it arc out and stab into the final mapping of snow.

At four he made another sandwich, the same sliced ham and two pieces of cheese. The weight he lost in the fall was inching back on, gathering at his middle.

A teal green Honda pulled up. It was pocked with rust and the hood was bent at its center, held down by twine, as if it had been run into a tree or sign. She sat hunched at the wheel, looking out, considering something. The car's exhaust hung in the cold air like a phantom behind her. She was slight. Even from the house he could see that. She had on a royal blue down coat. She was sitting in it, more than wearing it. She turned, squinting, making out the house numbers. He waved, unsure if she had found him there, in the window.

He liked her name, Caroline. It sounded of lost love and lace. He took her upstairs.

It was his old bedroom he was trying to rent. He'd moved into his parents' room, for the closets mostly. He'd had cable installed in the bedrooms, though she'd have to buy her own television. He showed her the convenience of the adjoining bath and stood with her at the window, pointing out the view through the trees, how you could make out the reservoir.

"Like there's a shortage of views around here," she said.

He wondered about her age. Twenty, maybe. She had red-brown hair that she wore down, not particularly tended, one side tucked behind her ear, the bangs cropped bluntly over mineral green eyes. She looked around the room as if it were a museum tour, gaze sweeping floor to ceiling, never touching anything, making little satisfied sounds. She was right. It was all trees and water around here, then a house, then a hill, and more trees and water again. But he'd always liked this particular view from his room, that it didn't look out on the yard or the building that had been his father's office.

He opened the doors to the master bedroom, feeling he was letting her know there was nothing to fear on the other side. He hadn't considered that a girl would respond to his ad, let alone someone near his age. This was Maine.

Downstairs she touched the wallpaper in the hallway, a fleur-de-lis print. "You sure this is your place?"

Then, walking by his mother's study, she stopped and asked if she could rent that room instead. He hadn't entered that room all winter. The rolltop desk was still open, the darning needles still piercing a half-wound ball of brown yarn. He wasn't sentimental about it. He just hadn't needed anything in there.

"You from here?" He asked at the study door, aware of the milky flesh of her hands, her neck, her cheeks, of what was bare.

"No."

"What brings you?"

"School."

"Where you going?"

"Any school will do." She tugged at the waist of her jeans out of necessity or nervous habit. "Look," she said, "this was as far as I could get from home."

"Oh."

"I'm not in trouble or anything. No one hit me. No one's looking for me. My dad knows I'm here. He'll send money if I need it." She put a hand on the pipe of the wood-burning stove and shook it, half-heartedly, as if to check the workmanship.

"Where's home?" He wanted to photograph her.

"California. I'm good for at least three months in advance. If you want it."

"I don't."

She spent the first night on the floor. He brought her a pillow and blanket, but she was already asleep, her head on a duffel bag, her grayed sneakers still on.

The next day they hefted his twin mattress down. She made up the bed in the corner behind the door. He asked her not to use the stove in the room. His mother had, but he had vague concerns about insurance and liabilities. He told her he'd ask the family lawyer, if that was why she wanted the room.

"Wasn't," she said. "It's cool."

She woke early every day, before the first light, left in her car and then returned around ten and went back to bed, behind the door. He took to looking for her car to see if she was in the house or not. In the evenings, sometimes, he saw her in the kitchen. She rarely cooked, just stood eating crackers over the sink, slurping juice. But there was only a half bath on the first floor and so she had to go upstairs to have a shower and that was how they bumped into one another, in the hall, Caroline in a towel.

Drew had slept with Louise Tate and Nora Lynes in high school. And then Emily in college. But everyone wanted to be with Nora Lynes. His strong jaw was an asset, his honest brown eyes, his thick hair, and his mother complimented his posture and manners, but Nora slept with him because he was quiet. She'd told him so. He hadn't known he was quiet until she'd told him so. And then he became cripplingly aware of it.

But he made an effort with Emily in college. He told her things he hadn't known he'd thought about until he said them to her. And they'd stayed in touch. She even came to town for his mother's wake and said he looked good, "given everything." He told her about the 200 mg of Wellbutrin, how he hadn't cried much at all and how he'd suspected his mother wouldn't live much longer than his father anyway. In fact, his mother had shown him the invitation to the Brannigan's Christmas party, a handsomely embossed card, and she'd said he should go. Not saying he should go with her, just that he should go, as if she'd known she wouldn't be alive. Emily asked if she'd done herself in, with a prescription or something. But that wasn't his mother. She was just going with her husband, Dr. Washburn, as if the last six weeks of her life had only been an extended version of her running in to gather her coat, the two of them hurrying off, the honored guests of a new sort of party. And he was okay. Really, he felt okay about everything. And he was through the bout of weeping spells that had settled in, like nimbus clouds, during that final semester, after Emily thought it best they just be friends.

"It's good you're doing so well," she said then.

"Not well," he said. "Just okay." And gave her a pursed smile.

He thought of calling Emily to tell her he found himself a roommate, like she'd suggested, but he didn't want her to hear in his voice that Caroline was prettier than she was. He'd learned that much, that women could know things without you saying them.

If it were a painting, it would be a Vermeer; that's how he thinks of his first photograph of Caroline. She was in his father's office, a building completely separate from the house, from where his father had maintained his medical practice. A small, four-room construction a dozen yards off. Drew had been at the window in his parents' room, eating an apple, feeling the day begin to close, looking, considering the structure, how to make sense of it—whether to knock it down or make a darkroom out of it—and then there was Caroline, standing in the yard, looking at the building, too. Almost with him. But then she started toward it. And then she opened the door and stepped inside. He picked up his camera in a militant way, as if in defense of his property.

There was the small reception area, two chairs, a couch, a door to the exam room, and through that room the door to his father's office. She was there, standing at his desk, a hand on the open leather schedule. He lifted the camera and took the picture before she turned toward him, before she could protest.

The window above his father's desk, the last of the day's yellow light, held her in its frame: that made it a Vermeer. And the way she'd put her hair up, away from her face. The iridescence of her skin made him think of the white wolves that emerged at the wood's edge in late winter, their eyes aglow with hunger, a counter brush of white against the wash of snow.

"I don't mind you photographing me," she said.

June. They were in the master bedroom, on top of the covers, the window open to the yard.

"Did you know about your dad doing abortions?"

"He was a regular doctor, too, for women." Drew saw himself foolishly gesture to his own privates. She was sitting up, looking at him, her mouth open, watching him talk. "I don't think it happened much." She'd let him touch beneath her shirt and he'd kissed her neck. He couldn't tell how much she liked it. She'd made the same small appraising sounds as when he'd shown her the house. He was surprised by her bones, how aware of her ribs and shoulders he was. But her breasts were small and firm, perfect in his hand. "He retired by the time I was ten. It was easier for women by then," he shrugged. "It wasn't dinner talk. But they didn't keep it from me either."

"Your mother knew?"

"She was a nurse."

"I bet it bothered you. I bet you hated seeing women walk back there alone, right by your room."

"I couldn't see from my room. And they weren't always alone. Why? Does it bother you?"

"Who came? Would the girl's parents come?"

"Sometimes. Or friends. There were older women, too. Sometimes men came with them. My mother would drive the ones who came alone."

"It doesn't bother me. I mean, you asked. I don't care." She sat up, reached back and refastened her bra. "Honestly, I'm all for it." She looked tired.

"You can stay up here," he said. Earlier, she put her hand to his when he went to remove his pants, stopping him. "If you aren't sleeping well downstairs."

She turned and smiled. That big, unexpected smile. "I know I can," she said.

In the afternoons, she drove around with him, helping set up the large format camera in front of the barns. Some days she seemed wound up, like a string had been pulled behind her, and she'd dance around in the fields, drift into the woods, then run toward him, making faces at the lens. But most days, she would settle and lay back wherever they were—in the open grass, the bed of his pickup, against the old stone well, the paisley couch—and let him kiss her for almost long enough, stopping him with the tips of her fingers from time to time, to ask about photography, about Maine, his parents. He'd answer as quickly as he could, then she'd close her eyes, as he leaned to find her lips again. He told her she knew him, better than even Emily had. He expected she would ask who Emily was, but she didn't.

One morning he woke before her and watched as she slept—the lilt of her nostrils, the fine hair on her face, the things a camera could catch, but that the eye rarely beheld. He stood at the foot of the bed feeling he'd actually grown taller.

In July, she sold her car.

He was in the kitchen, eating, of course—she made him feel like he was always eating—and he saw her walking up the drive, the fabric of her shirt briefly billowing on a breeze; a kite on a string.

"It's not about money," she told him, sitting at the table. He passed her half of his sandwich and to his surprise she picked it up, taking a small stiff bite. "I just like what we're doing here," she said, nodding, then chewing.

He wondered how far she'd had to walk back. He wasn't sure what she meant.

She still wouldn't have sex with him. But they'd been sharing the bed, him holding her, wrapped around her like a bear. Sometimes she'd reach back and stroke him and moan enough to let him drift into the belief that it was what they both wanted. But when he asked about her, anything at all—When's your birthday? *Funny you ask, it was yesterday.* What's your favorite color? What do you want to be?—all the things you ask on long summer days, half-clothed, beside someone you might love, she always answered in ways that made everything feel stifling. *Flesh color. Invisible.*

Then he asked about her father and she said he was famous. *Too famous to talk about.* Never meeting his eyes. The posture of a liar. His mother said lies were like sand. You could never keep hold of them and you'd find yourself digging deeper, trying to keep track, making a hole only big enough for yourself.

"I mean we could start a business or something. Shooting events, weddings." She was staring at the last of the bread between her fingers. "I could be your assistant. I don't need a car to be your assistant."

It was an idea. She'd ruined three rolls of film in a row when they were out in Randolph Forest the day before, flashing them in the changing bag. He still had his mother's Skylark in the garage. He could drive that. He hadn't asked for rent since May. He knew what Emily would say: *Be careful with yourself, Drew.* Like he was held together by cheap glue.

"You can use my pickup, when you need to."

The pickup was gone every morning, sometimes until two in the afternoon. There were mornings he left in the Skylark, driving up to Searsport. He told himself he wasn't looking for her, just a new subject. He felt something harden in his chest on one of these drives, some resolve.

"I need to know where you go." It had been dark for an hour. They were in bed. He muted the television: a cop drama that was making him anxious.

"Tough guy, eh?" She took the remote and aimed it at him, a gun, one eye closed. Damned cute. He'd watched her eat a pear earlier that night, knowing by the way she ate it that she hadn't eaten anything else all day.

"Caroline," he said.

She got up and started dressing. "Fine," she said. "You only had to ask."

She drove with one elbow on the open window, her head held in that hand, a look on her face that said he exhausted her. Fiery strands of her hair slipped out the window and rode the wind.

"I should take your picture in my truck," he said.

The house was in Bayside. One of the seasonal places, enormous, the kind that had its own name and a wraparound porch. Tennis courts ten paces out. Between the house and waterfront, a lap pool was left uncovered, lit up, dancing with marbled light. There was a paved driveway that led to the garage, the servants' drive, separate, quiet—this was the way Caroline had driven in, killing the headlights at the turn and backing into a clearing in the trees with an ease and practice that told him she'd done it a hundred times. There was a circular driveway in view now, covered in stones, coming off the cul-de-sac of houses they'd passed. He could see a few of the cars parked there: two Cadillacs, a Mercedes, a Lexus, all clean and shiny. The house was lit up, a party going on. Two dozen people. Women in floral dresses, men in shirts and ties.

"A whole lot of khaki in there," Drew said. His parents had brought him to a handful of these sorts of affairs. They always tired him, like a long swim in the ocean, short on oxygen.

Then Caroline started talking. She said the house belonged to a poet, a woman named Sasha Pynton. The property had been in her family for three generations. It had only been used as a summer home until Sasha inherited it. Supposedly, she lived there year-round now, writing in the winters and having friends stay with her for long stretches in the summer months. Caroline had read about her. Caroline's mother had been close to this woman, Sasha, a long time ago. "My dad said they were like sisters once. She even wrote poems about my mother." Drew wasn't sure what to say, what any of this had to do with anything, or where it left him, or why they were here, and then Caroline said, "She left when I was seven."

"Your mother?"

"Yeah, my mother. You could call her that." Music came on in the house, a swing band. "I started driving last summer with a friend."

"A girlfriend?"

"Yes, Drew. A girlfriend." She looked up, toward the house, watching. "But she was figuring things out, you know. We were good for a while, but she wanted to go home. I went back, too, but I couldn't stay. I physically couldn't."

A few of the people in the house were dancing now: limbs swaying, skirts twirling out. There was a sourness in Drew's mouth, his stomach, like the stench of rotting oranges. The downy hair on Caroline's upper arms was called *lanugo*—the same soft fur of premature babies. He'd read about it years ago, among his father's things, and he had looked it up again, just the day before, worried about her. It was what the body did to keep warm, to stay alive.

"You know that feeling after you stop running? How you still feel the rush, the memory in your limbs, but then it moves on, past you?"

"I don't know. I guess so."

"I didn't mean to end up here." She looked at her hands. "I just started driving again and then I was here. And you had an ad for the room and this house was so close." She looked over at him, a meek smile, as if checking whether he had heard her.

"So you're looking for her?"

"This is the only place my dad ever thought she might have gone."

"He never looked for her?"

"For what?"

Drew wondered how much of this was made up: what she was saying *and* what she'd been told. A life could hold so many lies, sometimes enough to keep it together. Sometimes not. "You come here? Every morning?" There was something off in his own voice, disbelief. He could see a blue vein along her cheekbone.

"Just until they're done with breakfast. You think that's pathetic, don't you? Sometimes I drive around Bayside, thinking I'll run into her. I don't care what you think, Drew. I realize that now. I thought it mattered to me. That's why I didn't tell you. 'Cause I thought I cared what you thought." She started the truck.

He pitied her. Even before he'd known about this house, about her mother, he'd pitied her. But now he was angry, too. They were back on Highway 3.

"Why in the morning?" he asked.

"If someone is staying there, they're most likely to come down in the morning. The rest of the day is a crapshoot."

"Has anyone seen you?"

"No."

"Have you seen anyone?"

"A few people. I saw this one woman with cropped black hair and I thought it might be her, that she could have changed her hair. Sometimes I think anyone could be her. But I'd know my mother, wouldn't I? I'd just know her."

"But what would you say? Have you thought about that?" He

heard himself. He sounded angry. She didn't look at him. Why was he angry?

She drove through a stop sign, then turned down the wrong road, then found her way out, thoughtlessly, like she'd made the same mistake a hundred times. She was more relaxed than he'd ever seen her. "Maybe I wouldn't say anything. Maybe I just want her to see me," she said and sat up a little straighter. "That's all."

He wanted her to be in here for him. That's why he was angry, because she wasn't.

The next morning the truck was gone, as usual, but by evening she had still not returned.

August. She'd only been his tenant, a companion. She was an adult. Wasn't she? Had they discussed her age? Unbelievable. Eight days and he could not come up with anyone to phone, to tell. He didn't know her last name. He considered reporting the truck. He even went to do the paperwork. Then couldn't. He sat outside the Bayside house in his mother's Skylark, her oiled leather seats, the sweet lilac perfume. "Be here," he said into the steering wheel, not deciding if he meant Caroline or Caroline's mother or his own. Then thinking, maybe. Maybe things do happen. Maybe Caroline and her mother were together. But he was also hoping not.

Sometimes Caroline had been in the bed beside him and he had not known it, she'd grown that thin. Then there would be a wrinkle of movement, the reveal of her red hair from beneath the edge of the pillow. She'd taken to sleeping on her stomach, with a pillow over her head, fully buried, barely there.

Late in August, two weeks into her being gone, he was standing in his mother's study, standing over the bed behind the door, and he swore he could see her there, beneath the heap of comforter and sheets. He could just make out her breathing. Or maybe it was his own. "I'll tell you every day, Caroline: I love you. Just stay with me. Be here with me." He slept on the floor beside the mattress that night, unwilling to lift the covers or reach to touch and learn that she, of course, wasn't there. He woke cold. The bed was empty, undisturbed. He found a thin notebook, a journal that had been tossed carelessly between the mattress and the wall.

On the first page he opened, he read the word *tongue* and quickly closed it shut. He checked the kitchen, the shower upstairs. Even walked through the office out back.

He opened the journal again only to read *Drew is a silly boy.* He could almost hear her laughing, a ghostly kind of echo as if she were somewhere in the house.

Silly boy. He walked around that entire day, calling himself that, unable to read any more. *Silly boy. Would silly boy like another sandwich?*

The night she returned, after three weeks gone, would be the only time he had sex with her. He swore this as it was happening, because she was more sick animal than woman now, down to bones and fur—and this was mixed into the act, his disgust. He had returned to her journal, read too much. He rolled from her and she lay there, shivering beside him.

"I'm sorry," she kept saying. "I'm sorry, Drew." She looked off, over his shoulder, as if waiting for him to look with her, to turn around, so she could steal things.

"I want the keys to the pickup," he said.

"Of course." She pulled closer, crying. "I'm messed up, I know. But I missed you, Drew."

Her being back, being back for him. That felt okay.

Late September. She was taking his Wellbutrin and it seemed to be helping. And he'd started her on calcium and iron supplements.

She left once in the middle of the night. He heard her digging in the drawers, looking for the keys. He did not stop her. He laid-awake until he heard her come in again.

She was at the kitchen table, frantically tapping one foot on the floor and twisting a plastic straw in her hands. She kept licking her lips.

"I thought I'd get us breakfast or something," she said. The table was bare. Sweat pilled on her forehead.

It was nothing, barely any effort for him to carry her up the stairs and bring her to the shower. Sometimes life was like this, like something you'd watched on television. And that made it easier somehow.

"It's okay," he said. "We'll try again."

She nodded and swore she would eat something, right after a nap.

They had not driven by the Bayside house since her return, but in late October she asked that he take her picture there, near the house. She wanted a Polaroid, to leave somewhere for her mother, he assumed.

No one seemed to be there. All the drapes had been pulled.

"Maybe she's gone to town."

"Maybe."

They were on the porch. Caroline only touched the knocker and the door swung open. Just like that. "Jesus," Caroline said. "Rich people." She had her hand to her chest, startled. "How do you get rich being so stupid?"

"Inheritance," Drew said.

Everything was covered in white sheets, a snowdrift. He had half a roll of film he wanted to finish before loading the Polaroid back onto the Mamiya. In the front room, there was a black baby grand piano left uncovered, the top still open. Drew touched a key. Caroline moved off somewhere.

In the dining room he photographed the massive chandelier, the cloaked table and chairs. His parents could have been to a party here. Only occasionally did they host their own parties, having grown weary of the occasional girl, the uninvited guest who would come back, his mother having to usher them off to her study, away from all the celebrants, her tone one of forced politeness, "If I'd known you were coming—." Drew was still a boy then, but he'd understood those girls, the look on their faces, how they wanted something already gone.

He heard Caroline crying in another room. He found her sitting at the base of the winding staircase. "She's not coming back," she said. "If she was ever here."

"You don't know that. They'll open the house again, in spring. We'll leave a note, so she knows—'

She stared at him, her mouth tight with detest. His simplicity, his hopefulness, all this false cheer. He too was sick with himself.

It hurt him sometimes, just looking at her. Her belly had grown distended. When she came to bed, she came completely naked and he'd go cold and hot at once. She seemed to enjoy his discomfort as much as she did her own hunger. He held her, but didn't touch her. He'd stopped pleading with her altogether, for fear of her laughing at him, making that forced yellow smile. If he so much as offered a cracker, she'd shake her head in a way that said he was stupid.

He took the Polaroid of her on the stairs. She was so slight in the frame you almost had to look for her. He went to leave the picture on the piano.

"Just keep it," she said.

November. No snow yet, but its dry warning was in the air.

They were out for a drive on one of those roads that dips and then rises at such an angle you can't be sure there is road on the other side: there is only the mild reassurance of what is supposed to be.

That morning, Caroline had heated soup and sipped at it. Since the photo in the Bayside house, she had been eating a little now and then. The bead of her pulse was still easily visible and her hair still pulled away in his fingers, but there was a renewed color to her cheeks and she was more talkative. The night before, she told him a story about when she was little, about a trick she and her mother used to play on her father, rearranging the things in his dresser, his tool box, just enough to confuse him. Drew had already read about this game in her journal, though there she had written that she thought there was something cruel about it, how she'd felt sorry for her father underneath the snickering, wanting as she did to laugh along with her mother, however unkind. *I hold on to all the wrong things,* she'd written elsewhere. *All the wrong people.* He had wedged the journal back between the mattress and the wall long ago, never mentioning it, unsure if she'd even care.

"Don't worry," she said to Drew. "I'd never play tricks on you."

They were driving over a different hill than any they had taken before. It was easy to get lost like that, the walls of pine, their thin stretch to the sky, making a mouse in a maze out of you. Drew was happy that day, happy with the changing leaves, their dying colors. He had an idea for a new image of Caroline: just her eyes, but with woods behind her, rich and out of focus. A dark bird would lift from a branch, leaving a swath of black in the frame, like smoke, something exorcised from her. How he was going to ensure the bird's flight he had yet to figure, but he needed to get out, to make more of their days together.

At the base of the hill, he looked over at her. She was wearing one of his old high school button downs, white, her blue down jacket over her lap. She had her forehead against the glass, her chin in her stemmed hand, her eyes skyward, searching the tree line.

"You ready?" he asked.

She nodded weakly.

She used to stick her head out in the wind, screaming as they crested over these hills. This day she only closed her eyes.

He gunned the truck. She gasped before they'd even reached the ridge. Then the tires left the road, lifting over the curve of the earth and then smacking down. She bounced up in the seat, and down again, as always. But then her hands fell limp into her lap.

There wasn't any shoulder on the road, but he pulled over.

He'd read about what to do. What was done in cases of cardiac arrest. He'd known this could happen. Breath, then compression, there was a count. He couldn't remember now, when it mattered. There were trees all around, so close and stoic, he had an urge to cry out for their help. Her hand; the sticks of her bones, the skin barely warm. Incomprehension seized him. A feeling familiar from his youth, the same delirium he felt at the parties of his parents' friends, the chinking of ice into glasses, the laughter, all the unbridled joy after such steely days. How confused he was by the sheer spectrum of emotion in so little time—what a single day could hold and how stuck in the in-between he felt.

Her ribs would fall to dust under his fists. Mortar and pestle.

He got out, leaving his door open, thinking how to lay her

down, whether he had a blanket, how to breathe, the count: it was two breaths, then some number of compressions. He was almost to her door when he heard her slide across the bench seat, the whisper of her jacket pulled behind her, the small crackling of leaves as she reached the other side of the road, her laughter. He stood outside the passenger window, watching. He watched her run deeper into the woods, her red hair flickering between the trees, the pale needle of her body disappearing, never looking back, never doubting that he would follow.

THE IOWA SHORT FICTION AWARD AND THE JOHN SIMMONS SHORT FICTION AWARD WINNERS, 1970–2013

Donald Anderson
Fire Road
Dianne Benedict
Shiny Objects
Marie-Helene Bertino
Safe as Houses
Will Boast
Power Ballads
David Borofka
Hints of His Mortality
Robert Boswell
Dancing in the Movies
Mark Brazaitis
The River of Lost Voices: Stories from Guatemala
Jack Cady
The Burning and Other Stories
Pat Carr
The Women in the Mirror
Kathryn Chetkovich
Friendly Fire
Cyrus Colter
The Beach Umbrella
Jennine Capó Crucet
How to Leave Hialeah
Jennifer S. Davis
Her Kind of Want
Janet Desaulniers
What You've Been Missing
Sharon Dilworth
The Long White
Susan M. Dodd
Old Wives' Tales
Merrill Feitell
Here Beneath Low-Flying Planes
James Fetler
Impossible Appetites
Starkey Flythe, Jr.
Lent: The Slow Fast
Sohrab Homi Fracis
Ticket to Minto: Stories of India and America
H. E. Francis
The Itinerary of Beggars
Abby Frucht
Fruit of the Month
Tereze Glück
May You Live in Interesting Times
Ivy Goodman
Heart Failure
Barbara Hamby
Lester Higata's 20th Century
Ann Harleman
Happiness
Elizabeth Harris
The Ant Generator
Ryan Harty
Bring Me Your Saddest Arizona
Mary Hedin
Fly Away Home
Beth Helms
American Wives
Jim Henry
Thank You for Being Concerned and Sensitive
Lisa Lenzo
Within the Lighted City
Kathryn Ma
All That Work and Still No Boys
Renée Manfredi
Where Love Leaves Us
Susan Onthank Mates
The Good Doctor
John McNally
Troublemakers

Molly McNett
One Dog Happy
Tessa Mellas
Lungs Full of Noise
Kate Milliken
If I'd Known You Were Coming
Kevin Moffett
Permanent Visitors
Lee B. Montgomery
Whose World Is This?
Rod Val Moore
Igloo among Palms
Lucia Nevai
Star Game
Thisbe Nissen
Out of the Girls' Room and into the Night
Dan O'Brien
Eminent Domain
Philip F. O'Connor
Old Morals, Small Continents, Darker Times
Sondra Spatt Olsen
Traps
Elizabeth Oness
Articles of Faith
Lon Otto
A Nest of Hooks
Natalie Petesch
After the First Death There Is No Other
Marilène Phipps-Kettlewell
The Company of Heaven: Stories from Haiti
Glen Pourciau
Invite
C. E. Poverman
The Black Velvet Girl
Michael Pritchett
The Venus Tree
Nancy Reisman
House Fires
Josh Rolnick
Pulp and Paper
Elizabeth Searle
My Body to You
Enid Shomer
Imaginary Men
Chad Simpson
Tell Everyone I Said Hi
Marly Swick
A Hole in the Language
Barry Targan
Harry Belten and the Mendelssohn Violin Concerto
Annabel Thomas
The Phototropic Woman
Jim Tomlinson
Things Kept, Things Left Behind
Doug Trevor
The Thin Tear in the Fabric of Space
Laura Valeri
The Kind of Things Saints Do
Anthony Varallo
This Day in History
Don Waters
Desert Gothic
Lex Williford
Macauley's Thumb
Miles Wilson
Line of Fall
Russell Working
Resurrectionists
Charles Wyatt
Listening to Mozart
Don Zancanella
Western Electric